v11-09	**DATE DUE**	4/01	
JUN 15 '01			
JUN 26 01			
DEC 1 0 2001			
1-15-02			
10-10-18			
GAYLORD			PRINTED IN U.S.A.

The Truth About the Cannonball Kid

The Truth About the Cannonball Kid

LEE HOFFMAN

Sagebrush
Large Print Westerns

Library of Congress Cataloging-in-Publication Data

Hoffman, Lee, 1932—
    The truth about the Cannonball Kid / Lee Hoffman
        p.   cm.
    ISBN 1-57490-332-2 (lg. print : alk.paper)
    1. Large type books. I. Title

PS3558.O346 T78 2001
813'.54—dc21   00-051005

Cataloguing in Publication Data is available from
the British Library and the National Library of Australia.

Sagebrush Large Print Westerns are published in the United
States and Canada by Thomas T. Beeler, Publisher, PO Box 659,
Hampton Falls, New Hampshire 03844-0659. ISBN 1-57490-332-2

Published in the United Kingdom, Eire, and the Republic of
South Africa by Isis Publishing Ltd, 7 Centremead, Osney
Mead, Oxford OX2 0ES England. ISBN 0-7531-6438-8

Published in Australia and New Zealand by Bolinda Publishing
Pty Ltd, 17 Mohr Street, Tullamarine, Victoria, Australia, 3043
ISBN 1-74030-295-8

Manufactured by Sheridan Books in Chelsea, Michigan.

CHAPTER 1

"WHY, ISN'T THAT NICE!" OLIVIA LACEY SAID SUDDENLY. "Ma'am?" Henry Caleb Lacey, Junior, asked his mother.

Olivia was perched in the big rocker beside the fire-place. Startled, she lowered her newspaper and peered over it at her son. She hadn't been aware he was in the room. Henry was like that. It was easy to overlook him.

He was a lanky gawky boy with good strong shoulders and an exceptionally blank face. At sixteen, he had such scant whiskers that he plucked them with tweezers instead of shaving them with a razor.

He was sitting on the floor by the hearth, whittling with the Barlow knife his mother had given him for his birthday yesterday. He aimed the wood chips into the cold fireplace. He kept missing. Bulky rag bandages encumbered the three fingers he'd sliced so far.

Olivia answered his question. "Your Uncle Ned is giving a temperance lecture in Independence next month."

"Are we gonna go, Maw?"

She shook her head. Independence wasn't a far trip and she thought it would be nice to see Ned again, but she definitely did not want to expose her only son to the evil influence of the city. Not even to hear a temperance lecture.

Olivia Lacey, nee Olivia Thrablow Oldcastle, was a woman of most high moral character. Entirely too high to suit the hired hands who came and went on the poor widow's farm with remarkable rapidity. She intended her son to grow into a pure and pious man, uncontaminated by

1

the moral squalor of the outside world.

Of course it had been impossible to protect him from certain sordid facts. Pigs littered regularly on the farm, and the milk cows had to be serviced if they were to stay fresh. Even so, she managed to keep Henry convinced that he himself had grown from a seed in the cabbage patch. True, Henry occasionally pondered this peculiar origin, but from his earliest days he had been trained to accept his mother's word without question.

"No," Olivia said. "We shan't go to Independence. I'll write your Uncle Ned and invite him here for a visit. Perhaps he'll speak at Sunday Meeting for us."

Henry sighed. He didn't really want to hear another temperance lecture. He'd heard plenty of them from Parson Fhew, from his mother, and from all manner of speakers at the church. Although he'd never even seen a drop of Satan's Brew, he'd signed pledge after pledge after pledge. What he wanted was to see a real honest-to-goodness city.

He sighed again and took another slice at his whittling stick. He cut his thumb instead. Sucking at the thumb, he said, "I didn't know I had an Uncle Ned."

"Don't talk with your mouth full," Olivia told him.

He removed the thumb and repeated, "I didn't know I had an Uncle Ned."

Olivia studied him over her spectacles. The boy was sixteen now. On the brink of manhood. She allowed to herself that it would be impossible to keep *all* of the crueler facts of life from him forever. If Ned came to visit, the truth might leak out. Perhaps it would be best if Henry were prepared.

Reluctantly, she admitted, "Your Uncle Ned was the black sheep of the family."

"Ma'am?"

2

"He—uh—he had—er—rambling ways. A handsome charming boy but wild. Wild. There were times I actually feared for his immortal soul. It's a relief to know he's finally found The True Path To Glory."

With that, Olivia Lacey smiled sweetly and keeled over dead.

The funeral was fun. Womenfolk from the neighboring farms brought all kinds of food and everybody fussed over Henry, showing him more attention than he'd had in his whole life up till then. It was almost like a church social, except for the sobbing and the burying. Henry couldn't make sense of the sobbing. According to the Parson, Olivia Lacey was in a far better world than the one she'd left. It seemed to Henry folks should be happy for her.

When it was all over, Parson Fhew announced that Henry must come stay with him and his family until suitable arrangements could be made. The Fhews had a rattailed forty acres of cotton and hemp over the rise a ways, and thirteen younguns.

The Parson loaded his missus, his younguns, and Henry into the wagon. He whipped up the mules, then turned to Henry and asked, "You have any kin, boy?"

Henry knew that his father was dead, and his father's father and mother were dead, and his mother's father and mother were dead, and now his mother was dead. He couldn't recall any other kin. For a moment, he felt terribly alone in the world. Then he remembered that last conversation with his mother.

Brightening, he told the Parson, "I've got an Uncle Ned."

"You got any notion where he might be?"

"Yes, sir. He's going to be in Independence next month giving a temperance lecture. Can we go, Parson?

3

Can we go, please?"

Missus Fhew spoke up hopefully. "It'd be a nice trip for the younguns."

The Parson frowned in thought. If they went, it would mean staying overnight. He calculated the cost of boarding his brood in the city and answered, "Independence is a Den of Iniquity, a Sodom and Gomorrah of the New World. No fit place for the Godly. Especially not for younguns. I'll write this Uncle Ned and tell him to come here. Besides, there's affairs to be settled."

It was about the answer Missus Fhew had expected.

Henry sighed. He wondered if he'd ever see a real city. He wondered what would happen when his Uncle Ned arrived. With assorted Fhew younguns clambering gaily over him, he sat morosely contemplating the fact that he had a future to contemplate. It had never occurred to him before to think past the spring planting or the next harvest.

A month with the Fhew family was no fun at all. The Parson felt the best thing for someone in mourning was a light diet and a lot of hard work. In view of Missus Fhew's cooking, Henry didn't mind the light diet, and he was accustomed to hard work, but the chores the Parson managed to line up for him seemed endless. With each new dawn's list of chores, he thought hopefully that perhaps Uncle Ned might arrive that day.

It was a bright, rather hot morning in the middle of May and he was on the barn roof, tacking down loose shakes, when he saw a buggy raising dust in the distance. He watched long enough to be sure it was headed for the Fhew farm, then looked around for someone to warn.

4

Parson Fhew was in the barnyard packing powdered bluestone into the thrushy hoof of a trotting horse he planned to trade off after meeting next Sunday.

Henry called to him through a mouthful of nails, "Sir! Parson, sir, there's company coming!"

"Don't talk with your mouth full," the Parson called back.

Henry spat out the nails and repeated his message.

Dropping the diseased hoof, the Parson hollered, "You go fetch the younguns while I tell the Missus!"

Henry scrambled down off the roof and hurried to the field where the older younguns were hoeing weeds while the younger ones wallowed in the dust. He managed to get them all rounded up and back to the house. Missus Fhew set them to scrubbing up, then told Henry to quick fetch firewood while she ground fresh coffee for the pot, and to hurry and make himself presentable.

By the time the buggy rolled to a stop in front of the house, the entire Fhew family was slicked and polished and ready to be presented. All were peeking through the curtains. The coffee was boiling over.

The driver of the buggy was a total stranger. He was a well-built man somewhere in his middle years. His suit was a respectable black, like the Parson's, but its neat cut and fit suggested custom tailoring. When he took off his tastefully conservative beaver to knock road dust from it, he displayed a thick thatch of dark hair, peppered with gray. His burnsides were close-trimmed, his chin clean-shaven. Replacing the hat, he climbed down from the buggy. He stood tall, with an air of quiet competent dignity.

All in all, as Missus Fhew commented, he was a fine figure of a man.

From the foot of the steps, he called a hallo to the house. His voice was deep and resonant and it boomed gorgeously, giving the Parson a twinge of envy.

The Parson opened the door.

The stranger made a small courtly bow that completely charmed Missus Fhew, and said, "I, sir, am Edward Jonathan Oldcastle. And you, I presume, are The Reverend Ezbai Fhew?"

"You presume right, Mister Oldcastle," the Parson said. "You're Olivia Lacey's brother?"

"I am."

"Henry Caleb," Missus Fhew whispered excitedly. "It's your Uncle Ned! Ain't he grand!"

Parson Fhew lined up his brood and introduced them all. Each little Fhew shook hands with the visitor, then departed to peel his good clothes and get back to work in the fields.

Once the parlor was cleared of excess Fhews, the Missus served coffee. Settled in the good chair, with his cup balanced on his knee, Uncle Ned asked after his sister's untimely demise.

The Parson explained that Doc Kimble, who lived over to Serenity, a good five miles away, hadn't seen the remains, but had announced with the utmost confidence that the cause of death was acute indigestion. There had been no need for the doctor actually to examine the corpse. Unless the deceased showed visible signs, such as a crushed skull or large bullet holes, Doc Kimble always concluded death was due to acute indigestion.

Shaking his head sadly, Uncle Ned spoke of various occasions when persons in the prime of life had passed on suddenly from the same cause. He advised a good tonic, morning and evening, to regulate the activities of the digestive system.

6

Henry sat listening, fascinated by the melodious tones of his uncle's voice. He was certain Uncle Ned's words were the ultimate in wisdom, and he was glad that every day as far back as he could remember, he had been dosed with two tablespoons of soothing syrup.

The Parson proceeded to describe Olivia Lacey's funeral in detail. Then, after discussing farming, prices, the weather, and the evils of alcohol, Uncle Ned inquired concerning Henry's inheritance.

At that Henry interrupted in a most unseemly manner. "The farm's awful fine, Uncle Ned! There's forty acres of bottom land, three milch cows, a score of hawgs, a mess of chickens, a real good house and sheds, and as pure a spring as ever you tasted from!"

"Excellent, my boy," Uncle Ned said with a satisfied nod.

The Parson said, "I'll give you nine hundred on the barrelhead for it."

Uncle Ned looked taken aback. "Surely such a fine farm is worth at least twice that amount."

"Well, truth is, prices is down bad," the Parson told him. "And the milch cows is going dry, and the hawgs got drop tail and blind staggers, and the hens ain't laying, and the house needs flooring, and the sheds needs new roofs, and the well's going putrid."

"That ain't so!" Henry protested. Startled by his own boldness, he added, "Sir."

"Shut up, boy," Parson Fhew said loudly and firmly. "This ain't none of your business."

Cowed, Henry slumped back into his chair.

Uncle Ned said, "Every day ships full of immigrants are arriving from all over Europe in search of good farm land in this great nation. I'm certain an ambitious

7

immigrant family would be pleased to pay as much as two thousand for the place."

"I wouldn't be so sure," the Parson drawled. "Them Dutchmen ain't stupid."

"Neither am I," Uncle Ned said. "If the place were offered up in St. Louis or Kansas City, it would undoubtedly bring a fair price quickly."

"Nine hundred's a fair price," the Parson insisted.

"However," Uncle Ned continued, "since you've been so kind in taking this poor orphaned boy into your home, I'd be willing to let you have it for a mere sixteen hundred."

"*Sixteen hundred!*" the Parson exploded. "That's pure plain robbery!"

"*Sir!*" Uncle Ned rose indignantly. He bowed coolly to Missus Fhew. Slapping his beaver on his head, he added, "Good day!"

"Hold on!" the Parson called at him as he stalked toward the door.

Uncle Ned paused and looked back.

The Parson grumbled, "Eleven hundred, and not a cent more."

"Fourteen hundred and not a cent less," Uncle Ned answered.

The Parson muttered something to himself, then said, "Twelve-fifty."

"In gold. On the barrelhead." Uncle Ned held out a hand to shake on the bargain.

"On the barrelhead," Parson Fhew agreed. He shook the proferred hand, then went to fetch a shovel and unearth his savings.

"Uncle Ned," Henry said tentatively. "I don't think I want to sell Maw's farm."

Uncle Ned looked sternly at him. "My boy, listen to

the advice of older and wiser heads. I am your only remaining kin. The trustee of your estate as it were. Put yourself into my hands. *I* know what's best."

"Yes, sir," Henry agreed.

"Henry Caleb," Missus Fhew said. "Go pack your belongings."

Warily, Uncle Ned asked, "Is the boy going somewhere?"

"Why, with you of course, Mister Oldcastle," Missus Fhew answered.

"One moment, please, madam. Not with *me!* I fear I have no place for the boy. I certainly can't drag him about with me in my travels. I have no wife to provide him with a mother's love and guidance."

"Travel would be good for him. He'd see the world. Get himself some larning. Hear them temperance lectures of yours."

"The boy needs proper formal schooling."

"He's had it. Three whole years. He can read and write and figger pretty as anybody in the county."

"But, madam—"

She pressed on. "He needs the kind of love only *blood* kin can give him. The kind of educating only a man like yourself can give him."

"What's the trouble?" Parson Fhew asked as he came trotting into the room, holding his cache box in his hands.

"Mister Oldcastle don't want to take the boy," his Missus told him.

Uncle Ned said, "I fear it is impossible. Totally irrevocable impossible."

The Parson harrumphed. He said, "It ain't possible. The boy can't stay on here. I got my own brood to tend."

"*I* can't take him," Uncle Ned said.

"Then I reckon we'll have to find somebody else as will," the Parson sighed. "Of course, if he don't go with you, I won't be able to buy the farm off you. Poor boy'll need it hisself to pay his keep. You understand me, Mister Oldcastle?"

Uncle Ned looked thoughtfully at the money box the Parson held. Then he looked thoughtfully at Henry. At last, he said, "Go pack your belongings, boy."

CHAPTER 2

SERENITY, MISSOURI, WAS THE BIGGEST TOWN HENRY had ever seen. It was the only town he'd ever seen. Two or three times a year, his mother had taken him there. Each time he was impressed. Not only was Serenity the county seat, with a two story courthouse, but it also had a railroad station. A train passed through town every other day. If the station agent put out a red lantern, the train would actually stop in Serenity.

Parson Fhew rode into town with Uncle Ned and Henry. They went directly to the courthouse. There, they indulged in various mysterious activities that resulted in Parson Fhew becoming the legal owner of the Lacey farm. That done, they headed back to the buggy.

Arriving at the buggy, Uncle Ned came to a sudden stop and gasped, "Oh, goodness!"

"Something the matter?" the Parson asked him.

"I absolutely must proceed on my lecture tour. I have several specific commitments and I should be loathe to fail even one. However, I cannot possibly reach Kansas City in time if I travel by buggy."

10

"Take the cars then."

"Yes," Uncle Ned said thoughtfully. "The train would get me there in time. But what of my fine rig and that magnificent steed between the shafts?"

The Parson eyed him slaunchwise. "Oh? You want to sell me your rig, huh?"

"Sir?" Uncle Ned looked as if such a thought had never crossed his mind. He said slowly, "I suppose I might just possibly entertain the prospect."

"Make it quick. Train's due in an hour. If you miss this one, there ain't another till day after tomorrow."

"Indeed? As much as it should sadden me to part with this excellent conveyance and the noble beast that has served me so well, it would seem a necessity. And it would certainly simplify your own problem of finding transportation back to your domicile."

"Might," the Parson allowed as he squatted to examine the horse's nigh fetlock.

When they had arrived at a price agreeable to both, Uncle Ned had Henry lift the luggage out of the buggy. There were only two pieces, Uncle Ned's calfskin traveling case and Henry's carpetbag.

"Mind you don't scuff the leather," Uncle Ned said as Henry set the cases on the walk.

Parson Fhew climbed into the buggy, clucked at the horse and headed for home.

Watching him go, Uncle Ned smiled.

The smile faded as he turned and looked at Henry. Shaking his head, he said, "What the devil am I going to do with *you*?"

Henry looked blankly back at him.

"Well, come along, boy. I'll think of something."

Uncle Ned parked Henry and the luggage on a bench at the railroad station, then disappeared. Henry sat

11

staring at the tracks. He was actually going to get to ride on a train. And then to see an honest-to-goodness city. He thought Kansas City might even be bigger than Independence, though he wasn't sure.

Uncle Ned reappeared. Without a word, he sat down next to Henry and pulled a little yellow-covered book from his pocket. Flipping it open, he began to read.

Henry stared at the book. After a moment, he said, "Uncle Ned, sir?"

"What?"

"That book."

Uncle Ned flopped the book closed over his forefinger and looked at the cover. The title was *Malaesky, The Indian Wife of the White Hunter.* The author was Sophia Winterbotham Stephens. It was a book he'd read several times before, and enjoyed every time.

He said, "What about this book?"

Henry told him, "My Maw always said all them little books like that there was lures of the Bad One to tempt and ensnare innocent souls into corruption."

"My boy," Uncle Ned answered. "These books are educational. One could live a thousand lifetimes, traveling to every corner of the earth, and never experience such adventures as one encounters between these saffron covers."

Confused, Henry said, "Ain't they evil, sir?"

"Evil, my boy? Indeed, what is *evil?* A phantom, a folly, a thought. Boy, evil is in the eye of the beholder. Nothing can corrupt the truly pure of heart."

"Nothing?"

"Absolutely nothing." With that, Uncle Ned returned to his reading.

Some three hours later the train puffed in and

wheezed to a halt. The engine, a Baldwin Tiger, had seen its prime before the Civil War and was long since due its pensioning out. Behind the tender, it hauled one baggage car, one passenger car, and a doghouse caboose, all as old as the engine itself.

Uncle Ned viewed the poor affair as one of those hopelessly outdated misfortunes of rural America. The coach floor creaked underfoot. The seats were too hard and too small for his frame. The carpeting was threadbare. The plush valances on the windows were hardly fit to feed starving moths. There wasn't even a clerestory to provide adequate ventilation.

To Henry, the train was an awesome marvel of the nineteenth century. The locomotive seemed a veritable demon from The Bad Place, sputtering sparks, puffing smoke and hissing steam. The coach was bigger than the house he'd been raised in, and unimaginably elegant, with carpeting on the floor and plush drapes at the windows.

Once under way, the whole affair rattled along at such a speed that Henry's head fairly spun. He gazed out the window as the scenery and hours flew by.

Uncle Ned read.

The afternoon was getting old when the locomotive gave an appalling toot and began to slow.

"What's the matter, sir?" Henry asked his uncle.

From the far end of the car, the conductor called, "Pintz!"

"We're coming into the station," Uncle Ned said. "Get the luggage."

"Sir?"

"Get the luggage. We're getting off here."

"At Pintz? But ain't we going to Kansas City? I thought you told Parson Fhew—"

"Never mind the Parson. We're getting off here."

"But Pintz ain't hardly even a town at all. Please, can't we at least go to Independence?"

"1 just came from Independence."

"Can't you go back?"

"My boy—er—what did you say your name was?"

"Henry Caleb Lacey, Junior, sir."

"My boy, I fear at the present my return to that charming metropolis might not be in our best interests."

"Sir?"

"It would seem I drove from Independence to that horrible Parson's place in a *hired* rig. The Independence constabulary can be rather bothersome about the most trivial indiscretions, as I had occasion to note shortly before I left their fair city. I think it best we depart this humble conveyance in Pintz."

"You didn't own that rig?" Henry said.

The train lurched to a stop. Suddenly Henry forgot about Independence and the rig. Clutching his stomach, he said, "Sir, I—uh—I think I'm gonna be sick."

"Hurry then," Uncle Ned suggested as he stepped into the aisle. "Bring the luggage and come along quickly."

Henry darted from the train and disappeared around a corner of the station house. Once he'd emptied his distressed stomach, he slumped to sit on the bottom station step. Resting his head in his hands, he groaned "I'm sorry, sir."

Rather sympathetically, Uncle Ned said, "Think nothing of it, boy. Such discomfiture frequently assails those unaccustomed to rail travel. What you need now is a good tonic."

14

"My Maw used to give me Doc Slattery's Soothing Syrup. Every night and morning."

"Excellent idea. Excellent formulation. I shall obtain a quantity anon. Wait here, my boy."

Henry waited. Uncle Ned was gone so long that it began to seem like he might never come back. But he returned at last, carrying several bottles of soothing syrup. He led Henry to the Pintz Lodging House and hired a private room for the two of them.

Inside the tiny room, Henry collapsed on the bed. Uncle Ned uncorked a bottle of soothing syrup and sampled it. With a smack of his lips, he handed the bottle to Henry.

"Drink up now, boy," he said.

Henry took a walloping gulp of the syrup. Only instead of soothing, it seared and scalded down his gullet. Sputtering, coughing, he managed to gasp, "Maw always gimme a spoonful in a glass of water."

"Oh. Of course. I should have realized—" Uncle Ned opened his traveling case and fished out a collapsible drinking cup. He poured water into the cup from the pitcher on the commode, then added the entire remaining contents of the bottle. "Here. Sip this slowly. Drink it all down now."

"Yes, sir."

The soothing syrup was still rather strong but Henry managed to empty the cup. Meanwhile, Uncle Ned finished off a bottle neat. They shared the third bottle.

By then Henry was feeling very drowsy. He stretched out with his head on the pillow and, smiling to himself, began to snore.

Satisfied that his charge would stay put until morning, Uncle Ned changed collars and tiptoed out to see what small pleasures the town of Pintz might offer a man with both time and money on his hands.

Henry woke the next morning even sicker than he'd been before. He was dimly aware of his uncle saying something about dog hair and dosing him with more soothing syrup. Then he fell asleep again.

The day—or two—or three—that followed were dizzy and dreamlike in his mind. He knew he'd bounced about in a buggy Uncle Ned hired somewhere. Then Uncle Ned sold the rig and loaded him onto another train. Dosed with more soothing syrup, he slept again. He didn't actually waken thoroughly until the moment Uncle Ned shook his arm and told him, "Come along now, boy. We're in Omaha."

CHAPTER 3

HENRY'S FIRST IMPRESSION OF OMAHA WAS OF complete confusion.

Trains hooted and puffed in the railyards. Cattle bawled and pigs squealed in the holding pens. In the streets, hooves clattered, wagons rumbled, teamsters shouted, and hawkers called their wares. An astonishing conglomeration of odors overhung them all.

The buildings were grand. Many were of brick or stone, and most of the ones Henry could see towered two, three, or even four stories above the streets. Some were pied from bottom to top with bright-painted advertisements.

The streets themselves were magnificent. They looked a hundred feet wide. Even so, they were jammed full. Drays and wagons, carts and buggies rolled past.

16

Men on horseback sauntered along. And everywhere there were people afoot.

All around Henry hats bobbed. Plug hats and flowered bonnets, wool hats and poke bonnets, animal-skin hats, high-crowned hats with brims like wagon wheels, and even a few Indian feathers here and there.

Henry had never imagined there were quite so many people in the whole world.

"Come along, boy. Mind the luggage," Uncle Ned said, striding into the midst of it all with the confidence of familiarity. Deftly, he wound his way through traffic and arrived safely at the far side of the street. He paused there to await his ward.

Henry scooted, darted, twisted, scurried and ducked. Finally, after fearsome difficulties, he arrived at his uncle's side.

"Hear that, boy?" Uncle Ned said to him.

"Hear what, sir?"

"The drum, boy. The drum."

Henry cocked his head as he listened. Above the clamor of the city, he made out the deep thud thud of a bass drum.

With another admonition to come along and mind the luggage, Uncle Ned started up the walk. Clutching the traveling cases, Henry hurried after him.

The call of the drum led them to a large vacant lot fronting on a side street. A crowd was gathering around a box wagon at the end of the lot. The wagon was tall, painted brilliant red and white, and trimmed with glittering gilt gingerbread woodwork. The tailgate was let down to make a platform at the aft end. On it stood a young man dressed entirely in white, except for the red bass drum he wore suspended from a strap around his neck. He had a padded stick in each hand and was

17

pounding slowly and steadily at the drum. Behind him a drape closed off the interior of the wagon. Lettered across it in crimson and gold were the words *Professor Whit's Wonder Elixir.*

Uncle Ned leaned toward Henry and whispered, "I'm going to have a little fun with an old friend. You wait here. Look out for the luggage."

"Yes, sir," Henry said uncertainly as his uncle disappeared into the crowd.

The man on the platform stopped beating his drum. Unhooking it from its strap, he set it aside. He raised his hands toward the spectators, gesturing for their attention.

"Ladies and gentlemen!" He gave his words a rhythmical lilt, as if he were about to burst into song. "You have no idea how happy I am to be here with you today. It has been—"

A voice from the crowd interrupted him, shouting frantically, "Professor! At last I've found you, Professor Whit!"

The Professor started like a shy horse. He looked like he might bolt. Then he almost smiled. He ended up shading his eyes and peering solemnly into the faces surrounding him.

"Sir?" he called.

The voice from the crowd was Uncle Ned's. "I've sought you to the very ends of the earth, Professor!"

"Won't you step forward, sir?"

Uncle Ned shoved through the platform. Accepting the hand the Professor offered, he climbed up onto the stage.

"What can I do for you sir?" the Professor asked.

Facing the crowd, Uncle Ned declaimed, "Two years ago, when my dear aging mother lay prostrate, I

18

purchased a bottle of your wonderful elixir for her. Within a week after consuming but one bottle of that miraculous tonic, she was not only on her feet, but she was plowing five acres a day. And that, mind you, without the aid of horse, mule or ox!"

The crowd burst into applause.

Uncle Ned took a bow in acknowledgment of their appreciation.

The Professor said, "It is my pleasure, sir, to be of service to humanity. It is to this end that I have devoted my very existence. It warms my heart to hear of your dear aged mother's recovery."

At the far side of the crowd, Henry frowned in puzzlement. He was certain his uncle's mother, his own grandmother, had been many years ago in her grave as the result of a bit of tainted pork.

"It was not to bring you these glad tidings alone that I have sought you out," Uncle Ned told the Professor. "Alas, a new and even more terrible calamity has befallen me and mine."

"Sir?" The Professor looked aghast.

"My dear lovely little wife had the misfortune to fall into a butt of malmsey recently. Now she lies prostrate with a severe dampness of the lungs. The finest medical practitioners of all Europe, and America as well, have pronounced themselves unable to do aught for her. Professor Whit, your wonderful elixir is her only hope. I *must* have a bottle at any price!"

The Professor reached into a box on the platform and brought out a small brown bottle. He offered it to Uncle Ned. "Take it, with my compliments."

Uncle Ned accepted the bottle, but he held out a coin in return. "I must pay you, Professor. I insist."

"If you insist," the Professor allowed. He took the

19

coin and announced to the audience, "This is a five dollar gold piece. The price of the elixir is but a mere dollar a bottle. I must get change for this good man."

"Nay, take it all!" Uncle Ned said with appropriate gestures. "Money in any amount is insufficient payment for the miracle contained in this small vial! All the money in the world could not pay you in full for the service your wonderful elixir has done for me and my loving family!"

From the audience, a man called, "Hey you, that there stuff really any good?"

"I assure you, sir, it is," the Professor answered.

"I'll give you four bits for a bottle," the man said.

Uncle Ned drew himself up indignantly. He addressed the prospective purchaser. "Sirrah, you insult the Professor with your paltry offer."

"Hold, sir," the Professor told Uncle Ned. "As you yourself have noted, my elixir performs incomparable services for mankind. How could I possibly dicker over a few miserable pennies when there may be a human life at stake?"

"I got a sick hawg," the man in the crowd informed them.

The crowd tittered.

The Professor told his prospective customer, "You shall have your elixir, sir, for only fifty cents. And my best wishes for the speedy recovery of the indisposed swine."

"That's not fair," another spectator called. "If he gets it for only four bits, I want it for four bits, too!"

"Me, too!" a woman shouted.

And then there was such a clamoring that it looked to Henry as if every man, woman and child in Omaha must be there begging for bottles of the wonderful elixir at half price.

20

The Professor held out his hands for silence. He announced, "Ladies and gentlemen, under the circumstances, I can see no alternative. Albeit the cost of concocting my marvelous elixir far exceeds the pittance you offer. I shall accede to your desires and sacrifice my stock today-and-today-only at great personal loss. While the supply lasts, I will permit all present to purchase Professor Whit's Wonder Elixir at a mere fifty cents a bottle!"

People crowded close, snatching bottles from the Professor as fast as he could hand them out, giving him hard money in return. Henry watched in fascination. He wished he had fifty cents so he, too, could take advantage of this unique opportunity.

Suddenly he realized his uncle was no longer on the platform. In fact, Uncle Ned was nowhere in sight. Luggage in hand, Henry began to push through the crowd, searching, calling, hoping.

Proud possessors of bargain bottles of elixir melted away from the mob. Almost the entire crowd dispersed and still Henry couldn't locate his uncle. He headed for the platform.

The last customer left. Squatting at the edge of the stage, the Professor fondled the little metal box he'd been dropping coins into.

Henry stepped up and asked; "Mister Professor, sir?"

"Sorry, my lad," the Professor said without looking up from his money box. "I'm afraid I just gave out the final bottle of my elixir. However, if you'll come back in a couple of hours, I'll have mixed up another batch."

"No, sir, I don't want your elixir—"

"*What!*" The Professor sounded completely taken aback.

He turned toward Henry. His hair and trim curly

moustache were the color of new copper and there were freckles across the bridge of his nose. He looked amused. Henry thought he might begin to laugh.

But instead, he said gravely, "The greatest tonic, stomach settler, blood purifier, bowel regulator, lung leavener, furniture renovator, paint remover, horse liniment and harness oil known to modern man, and *you don't want a bottle!*"

He made it sound like Henry was committing the eighth deadly sin.

Confused, Henry stammered, "I—uh—I been taking Doc Slattery's Soothing Syrup."

"No comparison, my lad. No comparison," the Professor said cheerily. Rising, he looked down his nose at Henry. Again he seemed on the edge of laughter. "Just try *my* elixir once and I warrant you'll never want to touch that third rate gut flush again."

With that, he tucked the money box under his arm and stepped toward the curtain that closed off the end of the wagon.

"Professor, please!" Henry called plaintively. "I'm looking for my uncle!"

The Professor answered, "I assure you *I* am not your uncle. Nor any other relative you may happen to have misplaced."

Suddenly the curtain fluttered and Uncle Ned emerged from the wagon. His coat was open, his head was bare, and his cravat was loose at his throat. He looked as if he had been relaxing quite comfortably.

Glowering at Henry, he said, "Boy, where on earth did you get off to?"

The Professor hooked a thumb at Henry and asked Uncle Ned, "He's yours?"

"I wasn't nowhere," Henry said. "I was waiting right

where you left me, like you told me."

Uncle Ned answered the Professor. "A bequest of my late not-very-lamented sister, Olivia, I fear."

"What's he worth?"

"He *was* worth forty acres of rather good Missouri farmland, but alas the boy has run through his entire inheritance already."

"Sir?" Henry said.

Uncle Ned kept right on talking to the Professor. "I fear the poor impecunious youth is now totally in my charge."

"What did you charge to take him in charge?" the Professor said.

Uncle Ned lifted a brow at him, then admitted, "Twelve-fifty in gold."

"Not bad. Come on inside and we'll tap the admiral."

Dragging the luggage along, Henry followed them into the wagon.

CHAPTER 4

INSIDE, THE PROFESSOR'S WAGON WAS A COZY LITTLE room with a shuttered window in each side wall. The walls were whitewashed and chintz curtains hung at the windows. Against one wall there was a rather wide bunk bed. Against the other was a row of waist-high cabinets. On the cabinets there sat a camp stove, a basin and pitcher, a clutter of personal effects and three tapped kegs. Boxes of bottles were stacked in the corners.

The Professor took three agateware cups from a cupboard. He drew each about half full of pale liquid from the middle keg and offered one to Uncle Ned.

"Is this the same stuff you use in the flukum?" Uncle Ned said.

"It is. The very best home-stilled corn singlings available in these environs."

"*I* never used anything less than doublings in *my* elixir."

"I know. That's your shortcoming, Ned," the Professor said, trying to suppress his grin and seem solemn. "You're generous to a fault. You cut your profit to a mere sixty or seventy percent using such lavish ingredients. I assure you, as singlings go, this is excellent stuff. I drink it myself."

"You'd even drink your own flukum," Uncle Ned answered with similar mock solemnity as he took the cup.

"What's flukum, sir?" Henry asked.

"Any liquid concoction, such as an elixir," Uncle Ned told him.

"What's singlings?"

The Professor said, "Whiskey."

Uncle Ned sampled the contents of his cup. He nodded and allowed, "Adequate, I suppose."

Henry gaped at the sight of his own uncle—Uncle Ned The Temperance Lecturer—imbibing strong spirits.

The Professor offered the second cup to Henry.

"No, sir! I don't want no truck with no hard likker. I know all about it. It's the Tool Of The Bad One for bringing folk into sin. I won't touch nothing with no alcoholic spirits in it!" Henry gave a very definite shake of his head.

The Professor lifted a brow in amused query. "I thought you mentioned indulgence in Slattery's Soothing Syrup."

"Oh, I drink that all right. But I don't use nothing with no alcohol in it. My Maw learnt me not to. I took The Pledge a lot."

24

The Professor turned his look of question toward Uncle Ned.

Smiling, Uncle Ned told Henry, "My boy, your attitude toward the Demon Rum and his relatives is most commendable but rather immoderate. The sin of alcohol is in excessive consumption thereof. Taken temperately, it is the cup that cheers. If you would be of good cheer, drink up."

The Professor said, "Lad, except for a dash of bitter herbs, a mild opiate, and a quantity of water, there is no major difference between Slattery's and the contents of this cup."

"There's spirits in Slattery's Soothing Syrup!" Henry gasped.

The Professor nodded.

Uncle Ned said, "In moderation, alcohol is a most remedial specific. It is man's best friend. I know. After all, am I not an exceedingly respected lecturer in the field of alcoholic temperance?"

"That's your line now, Ned?" the Professor asked him.

He nodded.

"Good money in it?"

"Not very." Uncle Ned paused to take a long swallow from his cup. "Perhaps you'd best water the brew for the boy. After all, he's inexperienced, except in soothing syrup."

"Certainly." The Professor turned and drew liquid from the end into the cup. He smiled pleasantly as he held the end keg into the cup. He smiled pleasantly as he held it out to Henry. This time he was not joshing or mocking. "If you don't want it, don't take it."

"Indeed," Uncle Ned agreed. "But if you don't try it, I promise someday you'll rue your reticence. I iterate,

25

alcohol is actually man's best friend."

Henry supposed his uncle knew best. He accepted the cup and sipped cautiously from it.

No claps of thunder ensued. No fiery apparitions of The Evil One appeared. Nothing untoward happened at all. Rather surprised, Henry sipped again. He found the taste of the liquid warm and pleasant. He seated himself on a box in a corner and took yet another sip.

Uncle Ned glanced around the wagon, giving his expression an exaggerated significance. Tongue well in cheek, he said, "Don't tell me you are domiciled in solitary seclusion these days?"

"At the moment. She ran out on me in Julesburg," the Professor admitted. He settled himself cross-legged on the bunk, facing its middle. Opening his money box, he dumped its contents onto the blanket in front of him. He ran his fingers joyfully through the coins and added, "I'll find me another soon though."

"Indeed you will," Uncle Ned said. He started to sit down on the bunk.

The Professor made a shooing gesture, suggestive that Uncle Ned place himself at the far end of the bunk. "Keep your fingers off the coin."

Uncle Ned feigned injured innocence as he moved over. "Clarence, my boy, would you cast aspersions on your erstwhile mentor?"

"Of course," the Professor answered cheerfully. His hands shuffled the coins into neat little stacks of five dollars each—without any apparent help from the Professor, whose eyes and attention remained on Uncle Ned.

"Ned," he said.

"Yes?"

"Please don't call me Clarence."

"It's a perfectly respectable name."

"You know I despise it."

"You've done your best to sully it," Uncle Ned said.

The Professor grinned in agreement. He said, "You gave me rather a start out there, Ned, shouting at me like that. For a moment I thought you were a lawman. Or an irate father."

"You picked it up well enough," Uncle Ned said with a chuckle.

"Yes, I did, didn't I? But I have to admit I had a bad moment. A butt of malmsey, indeed."

Seated in the corner, Henry had been sipping steadily at his drink. Most of it was gone now. He felt very warm and pleasant and puzzled. He asked, "Uncle Ned, sir, what was all that talk about Grandmaw and your poor sick wife and all?"

"Once upon a time, my boy, I was in the same profession presently pursued by our friend here." Uncle Ned indicated the Professor. "At that time, this callow youth was employed as my assistant. We found it aroused the interest of our audience if we opened each pitch with a small theatrical performance similar to that which you observed today."

"Only then I was the shill and Ned was the pitchman," the Professor added.

Frowning uncertainly, Henry said, "You mean it was some kind of *play-acting?*"

Uncle Ned nodded.

"But play-acting's evil!"

"Heavens, my boy! Whatever gave you such a notion?"

"My Maw said so. So did Parson Fhew."

"Small narrow minds," Uncle Ned said.

The Professor suggested, "With lives to match."

"Undoubtedly." Uncle Ned looked at Henry with rather amused sympathy. "My boy, in your youthful innocence, you have been badly misled by those petty puritanical prudes. But fear not. I shall see to your proper re-education."

"Indeed he will," the Professor said with a grin. He gestured at the cup Henry had almost emptied. "Care for another?"

"Thank you, sir." Henry gave him the cup.

The Professor refilled it, then refilled Uncle Ned's and his own. Seating himself on the bunk again, he picked up a handful of coin and let it filter through his fingers.

Uncle Ned drank, sighed, and asked conversationally, "Going to be in Omaha long?"

"I plan on pitching here again tomorrow night, then pulling out Sunday morning."

"Going anywhere in particular?"

The Professor shrugged. "Wherever the Fates may waft me. As long as it's this side of the Mississippi, of course."

"Of course."

"Why only this side, sir?" Henry asked.

"I'm afraid there are some—ah—difficulties back East that I'd prefer not to encounter," the Professor said.

Uncle Ned told Henry, "He means wives."

"Wives?"

The Professor nodded. "Alas, several of them. Entirely too many."

"In my own personal opinion *one* would be entirely too many," Uncle Ned said. "Clarence, why don't you join the Latter Day Saints?"

The Professor looked interested. "Is there money in Mormonism?"

"Around Salt Lake City there would seem to be. In

28

any case, it should alleviate your marital difficulties."

"Hardly! Believe me, Ned, I'd prefer not to be married to *any* of the ladies in question. I am appalled by the mere thought of being married to *all* of them." The Professor's tone was cheerfully rueful. He rose to refresh his drink.

"Indeed," Uncle Ned said, holding out his own cup for a refill. "I well comprehend your attitude toward your connubial encumbrances. Marriage is an unfortunate state for the male of our species. A dire pitfall one must always be alert against. It is the supreme joy of my own experience that I have never succumbed, and the ultimate ambition of my existence that I shall continue eternally in my singularly blessed state."

"I wish you success," the Professor said as he turned away from the keg. Holding a cup out to Uncle Ned, he added, "Put it back, Ned."

Uncle Ned sighed, mocked an expression of pained exasperation, and returned the handful of coins he'd pilfered from the pile while the Professor's back was turned. Accepting the drink, he said, "I think this will be my last for the moment. When I leave here, I want to consult a few local churchmen and arrange some temperance lectures. I'd best not have too intense an aura of John Barlycorn about me when I do."

"Then you don't already have engagements here?"

"No, my decision to grace this fair city with my presence was rather sudden."

"Horses, women, or gambling?"

"A little horsetrading in Missouri. Besides, I thought the boy here would profit from travel."

"I don't think you ever told me his name."

Uncle Ned looked at Henry. "Boy, what did you say your name was?"

"Henry Caleb Lacey, Junior, sir," Henry said. His words slurred slightly. He felt rather sleepy.

"My pleasure, Henry." The Professor gave a nod. He picked up one stack of coins from the bed, put it in his nigh pocket, picked up another for his off coat pocket, then produced a leather pouch and poured in the rest.

"Clarence," Uncle Ned said. "I fear you've failed to return my five dollar gold piece."

"What five dollar gold piece?"

"The one I rendered to you in the course of our performance."

"You gave me a five dollar gold piece?"

"Yes indeed I did. My *brass* one, Clarence."

"Oh. Brass." The Professor tugged a coin from his vest pocket and flipped it to Uncle Ned. "I do wish you wouldn't keep calling me Clarence."

"Of course. How rude of me."

"Care to help me mix up another batch of flukum?"

"I'm afraid we'll have to be running along now. Have to locate those churchmen," Uncle Ned answered.

The Professor suggested, "Come back after the last pitch tonight. We can have a decent dinner at Fabley's, then visit a few points of interest."

"Indeed! Excellent idea. I'll stow the boy and meet you here."

"Why not bring him along?"

"I don't know," Uncle Ned said doubtfully. "He'd likely cramp our style."

"Please, sir?" Henry said hopefully. "Please can I go."

The Professor grinned. "You said you plan to give him a proper education. Why not start now?"

"Perhaps. Well, we'll see. Come along, boy. And bring the luggage."

CHAPTER 5

HENRY HAD NEVER BEEN IN A RESTAURANT BEFORE. HE gazed around Fabley's, awed by the ranks of tables, each spread with a white cloth and illuminated by an overhead Rochester lamp. At the tables, gentlemen in fine suits and linen collars and ladies in plumed bonnets and ruching collarettes delved into heaping plates of exotic fare. Waiters moved about carrying trays with more fascinating foods.

Along one wall, set off from the dining room by a row of pillars and a lot of potted plants, there was a bar. Men bunched up to it, swigging an assortment of spirits. Some puffed cigars. Others chawed and spit into the gleaming brass cuspidors spotted abundantly along the floor.

Uncle Ned and the Professor strolled up to the bar. They made space for Henry between them. As he slid into it, Henry asked, "This ain't a Den of Iniquity, is it.

"Why, whatever gave you such a notion?" Uncle Ned said.

Henry shrugged.

Uncle Ned called the bartender and told him, "Two Martini Gins here. A brandy and water for the boy. Long on the water. He's young yet."

Nodding and smiling, the bartender set them up.

Henry took a test sip of the drink that was handed to him. Pleased by it, he took a hearty swallow.

"Hold, my boy, moderation," Uncle Ned cautioned. "I've no desire to abbreviate the pleasures of this evening in order to carry you home to bed at an unseemly early hour."

"Yes, sir." Dutifully, Henry took a very small sip.

Uncle Ned turned to the Professor. "Speaking of women, did you perchance indulge your propensity for matrimony with the one who left you in Julesburg?"

"Never! I've sworn off marriage altogether. I found it leads to annoying complications."

"Wise. Wise, indeed."

"It's all a snare and a delusion, Ned. Judith was her name. The raven-haired Judith, and as lovely a creature as you can imagine. But a vile senseless squandering spendthrift possessed by the green-eyed monster. Should I so much as glance at another woman in her presence she—she—uh—er—" The Professor's voice faded as he turned to give his total attention to something in the dining room.

Peering through a potted rubber plant, Henry spotted the object of his attention. A man in a derby was escorting a young woman across the room. She noticed the Professor and her very pink lips curved into a bit of a smile. Her eyelids fluttered.

Reaching an empty table, her escort pulled out a chair for her. When she sat down in it her back was to the Professor.

Sighing, he returned his attention to Uncle Ned. "You were saying?"

"The price of rice in China is exorbitant this season."

"Yes, indeed. Uh—er—rice in China?"

Uncle Ned chuckled. "Clarence, my boy, there is a single fatal flaw in your otherwise sterling and impeccable character."

"Preposterous, sir! And I do wish you wouldn't keep calling me Clarence."

Discovering his glass empty, Uncle Ned hailed the bartender for another round. Fresh drinks in hand, he and the Professor fell into a discussion of the medicinal flukum business. Suddenly, the Professor's voice trailed off as another young woman passed by.

"Come, boy," Uncle Ned said to Henry. He motioned toward the dining room. "Let us be seated and partake of viands."

"Sir?"

"Come along, boy. Let's eat." Uncle Ned stepped away from the bar.

Henry asked, "What about the Professor, sir?"

"He'll join us in a moment."

They settled at a table and a waiter appeared. Uncle Ned ordered beefsteaks all around. The waiter disappeared. The Professor arrived.

"A pretty little thing?" Uncle Ned asked him as he took his seat.

"Lovely. But attached."

"Oh well, you'll find another."

"I always do."

When the waiter returned with their dinners, Henry discovered himself facing a plate of food such as he'd never seen before. The steaks his mother had occasionally prepared had been pan fried into leathery crinkles. The piece of meat he now sampled lay on his tongue almost melting of its own accord. The vegetables were pert and crisp instead of limp and greasy. The breads were curiously soft and pleasant. He devoured all avidly.

Uncle Ned and the Professor dined leisurely. They topped off the meal with cigars for themselves and brandies all around. Then they shared the bill and sauntered into the night.

Henry was surprised to discover that, at an hour when he would normally be asleep and under the impression all the world was likewise, the streets of Omaha were brightly lit and bustling with people.

The establishment Uncle Ned led them into resembled Fabley's in layout. There were tables and along one wall, a bar. But this place wasn't so clean and fancy as the restaurant, and it didn't smell as good.

At one end of the room, on a raised platform, a man sawed at a fiddle while another pounded on a piano and a third beat a drum. Glasses and coin clinked. The only women present were moving among the tables delivering drinks.

Henry had heard of female waiters. Parson Fhew had mentioned them as one of the Ornaments of the Sodoms and Gomorrahs of the New World.

As they settled themselves at a table, Henry leaned toward Uncle Ned to ask anxiously, "Is this a Den of Iniquity, sir?"

"Of course not!"

A woman waiter stepped up to take their order. Henry discovered that her skirt showed not only button-booted ankles but black-stockinged calf as well. The discovery gave him a very strange feeling.

Uncle Ned ordered drinks. The Professor pinched the waitress in an unmentionable place. Giggling, she dashed off. In a moment, she was back with the drinks. As soon as she'd set them on the table, the Professor wrapped an arm around her waist and pulled her into his lap. They both laughed. He nibbled her ear.

Henry had that strange feeling again, even stronger this time.

The waitress rather reluctantly broke away from the Professor. As soon as she was out of earshot, Uncle Ned made a comment to the Professor, using a word Henry had never heard before. The Professor grinned and said he hoped so.

Henry gulped nervously at his drink and pondered the new feeling he'd discovered.

The music stopped. A man with bright red garters on his shirtsleeves mounted the stage and made an unintelligible announcement. Customers moved away from the bar to get clear views of the stage. One of them managed to step on Uncle Ned's foot.

Uncle Ned yelped in pain.

The stranger began to apologize profusely. From his unfamiliar accent, Henry guessed him to be a foreigner.

The Professor cocked an ear, then said, "Excuse me, sir, but you're a Philadelphian, aren't you?"

"How on earth did you know that?" the stranger asked.

Before the Professor could reply, Uncle Ned answered in his behalf, "He has second sight."

"Second sight!" the Philadelphian exclaimed. "How wonderful! I'm a serious student of spiritualism myself. In my childhood, I actually saw the Fox sisters. Very impressive!"

On stage, the waitresses had lined up in a row. As the music started, they began to bounce, kicking in unison. They showed a great deal of leg. Over the rim of his glass, Henry peered at them, then at the foreigner from Philadelphia, then at the dancers again. That funny feeling was back. A very pleasant feeling, but a little frightening. He clutched the glass with both hands. Even so, it trembled.

"Perhaps I might buy you gentlemen a round of drinks?" the Philadelphian suggested.

"Our pleasure, sir." Uncle Ned motioned for him to sit down.

He did, and introduced himself as Samuel Fairweather. Uncle Ned answered with his own name, then introduced the Professor as The World Famous Professor Richard Clarence The Third of The International Spiritualistic Institute of St. Louis.

"I'm honored, sir," Mister Fairweather said to the Professor.

But the Professor was completely preoccupied by the display on the stage.

In explanation, Uncle Ned said, "He's in a trance."

"Oh!" Mister Fairweather was duly impressed.

"It can happen quite suddenly. Any time. Any place," Uncle Ned expanded, taking pleasure in the process of creation. "It just comes over him. A contact with Other Worlds. Occasionally the revelations he receives are amazing."

"Fantastic," the Philadelphian said.

"He's the Seventh Son of a Seventh Son, you know."

"Uncle Ned, I didn't—" Henry began.

Uncle Ned cut him short with a swift kick under the table.

Hopefully, Mister Fairweather asked, "Are his revelations ever of—ah—*commercial* value?"

"They might be," Uncle Ned allowed. "But it is against the Professor's high moral principles to employ his talents for his own selfish financial gain. Were he willing, he could easily be the wealthiest man in the world today. However, he insists that his peculiar abilities be put to the service of others. A truly noble spirit."

"Truly," Mister Fairweather agreed.

Uncle Ned continued, "As it is, the poor lad barely subsists on a meager salary subsidized by the paltry contributions of miserly ingrates who have profited enormously by information received through his revelations."

"Is that so?" Mister Fairweather gazed at the Professor in speculative admiration. The Professor continued to gaze at the dancing waitresses.

Tentatively, Mister Fairweather asked Uncle Ned, "Do you suppose it might be possible for the Professor to consult with me concerning an investment I have in mind?"

"Perhaps." Uncle Ned made it sound doubtful.

"I'd gladly pay him."

"Sir! Professor Clarence never accepts payment. Pecuniary consideration is most alien to his character. However, I do suppose that if you'd care to contribute to the Institute, he'd have no objection. Just what is it you have in mind?"

"You might say the stock market." Mister Fairweather chuckled slightly. "I'm interested in a herd of cattle."

Uncle Ned politely echoed the chuckle, and said, "Tell me more."

"It's this way. There's a demand for beef back in Philadelphia and there's beef to be bought on the hoof in Omaha. I looked at some cattle belonging to a man named Slaughter over at the yards this afternoon. Good beef. He's asking thirty-five hundred for the lot. I've got the cash in hand. In my hotel room, in fact. But at that price, plus the costs of handling and shipping, I'd barely clear five hundred profit."

Henry did some quick counting on his fingers under the table. At a dollar a day and found, it would take a good hired man well over a year of hard work and steady saving to get that much cash together.

"A paltry return on your investment, indeed," Uncle Ned said sympathetically.

"This is my question," Mister Fairweather continued.

"Should I buy now at Slaughter's price, or hold off for a better deal? Will the price of beef in Omaha be rising or declining in the immediate future?"

"A very good question," Uncle Ned told him. "I shall take it up with the Professor. However, I shan't have an answer for you until tomorrow at the soonest. How can I contact you?"

Mister Fairweather took out his card case. He wrote the name of the hotel on the back of a card and handed it to Uncle Ned. Anxiously, he asked, "You will be in touch with me?"

"I promise, sir." Uncle Ned pocketed the card. "On the morrow."

"Thank you, sir! Thank you!"

The waitresses gave their final kick, took a bow, and returned to serving drinks. The Professor's attention returned to his companions. He gave them a cheery hello and told the Philadelphian, "I'm afraid sir, I didn't catch your name."

"Samuel J. Fairweather. Excuse me, Professor, but your trance—was there any revelation—perhaps something about the price of cattle?"

"Ah yes, my trance," the Professor said slowly, eyeing Uncle Ned for a cue of some kind.

"On the morrow," Uncle Ned told Mister Fairweather. "I promise you, sir, you'll have your answer then. Now, I fear you must excuse us."

"But your drinks. I was going to order—"

"Alas, we cannot take that pleasure with you. We must see this lad home to bed." Rising, Uncle Ned gestured at Henry. "Come along, boy. Professor."

Outside, the Professor asked, "What was that all about?"

"A pending business deal."

Henry asked, "Couldn't we just have stayed for them drinks, sir?"

"Timing is of the utmost importance in such matters, my boy," Uncle Ned told him. "We must now allow the fish time to contemplate the bait."

The Professor shook his head in denial. "You wanted to get out because you didn't want me to find out what you're up to and try to cut myself in."

"Would I do a thing like that, Clarence?" Uncle Ned said.

Henry asked, "Do I *have* to go home now?"

"Of course not, my boy. Come along. We'll find another haven of entertainment."

"You wouldn't cut out an old friend, would you, Ned?" the Professor said hopefully.

Uncle Ned walked away.

With a couple of fast steps, the Professor caught up. He threw himself wholeheartedly into a discussion of the merits of remembering old friends and the advantages of a reliable partner in an operation of magnitude. It was rather a one-sided discussion. Uncle Ned simply ignored him.

Henry trotted along behind, swaying somewhat under the burden of strong spirits he'd consumed.

CHAPTER 6

SHOVING OPEN A BATWING DOOR, UNCLE NED LED HIS entourage into another establishment similar to the last, except that this was smaller, dirtier and smellier. The aroma of the stockyards was even stronger inside than out. It seemed to be coming from the customers.

They were mostly rough looking men in coarse

clothing. Many of them packed handguns on their hips. All seemed to be wearing high-heeled boots with large jangly spurs.

There was no stage here, just a mechanical piano plinking away at the far end of the room. The noise of the customers drowned it out.

The tables were bare wood, ornamented with whittled initials and various stains. Flies lay about, some alive, some dead, some uncertain. At a few of the tables men were sitting and drinking. At others, they also indulged in a pastime involving pieces of printed pasteboard and stacks of coins.

Leaning close to Henry, the Professor whispered, "Now, *this* is a Den of Iniquity."

Henry looked around, duly impressed and a little frightened.

Uncle Ned ambled to the bar. He collected a bottle and three glasses and carried them to an empty table. As he poured, he warned Henry, "This is a more potent brew than you've been imbibing heretofore. Sip it slowly and mind, it may burn a bit going down."

"Yes, sir."

"As I was saying—" the Professor began.

Uncle Ned shoved a glass toward him. "Drink up, Clarence. And please find a new topic of conversation."

The Professor took a drink, then took a small box from his coat pocket. From it, he withdrew a stack of pasteboards like those in use at the other tables. He ruffled them, divided the stack in two, then merged them in a graceful motion that intrigued Henry.

"A new topic of conversation," he said to Uncle Ned.

Henry asked, "What are those things?"

The Professor looked surprised. "Playing cards."

40

"For gambling?"

"Yes," Uncle Ned said with rather a strange sigh.

"Gambling games is the Bad One's devices, ain't they?" Henry asked.

It was the Professor who replied. Mimicking Uncle Ned, he said' "Not in moderation, my boy. Moderation removes the onus of evil from all things. Gambling is an incomparable intellectual exercise. It stimulates a man's wits and improves his mental alertness. Develops competitive keenness. Eh, Ned?"

"You are the veritable Serpent Himself, Clarence," Uncle Ned said, gazing at the cards that danced between the Professor's fingers.

"A simple matter of moderation. Will power. Self-control," the Professor said. "Seven-up, Ned?"

Sighing, Uncle Ned poured another drink. He emptied the glass. Putting it down, he eyed the cards. Finally, reluctantly, slurring a little, he said, "Deal, you Son of Satan."

"Uncle Ned, sir," Henry said. He too slurred some-what. "I don't think you ought to call the professor names."

"What?" Uncle Ned scowled at the boy.

The Professor looked astonished.

"He's my friend," Henry said. "I think he's nice."

"*Nice?*" Uncle Ned said.

The Professor said, "*Me?*"

Henry nodded solemnly.

Uncle Ned gave the Professor a look of exaggerated sternness. Suppressing a chuckle, he said, "Sirrah, what devilish wiles have you employed to beguile my poor youthful ward? What hellish evils do you aspire to lead him into?"

The Professor assumed an air of injured innocence.

41

"You're the one who's been leading. I've just been following along."

"Yes indeed! Following along, imbibing my spirits." Uncle Ned held up the bottle. "Enjoying my hospitality and all the while alienating the affection of my only close kin. You, sirrah, are a cad."

"Have I ever denied it?"

"I'll allow you that. For a scoundrel and scalawag, you are more or less an honest man. As men go."

"You flatter me," the Professor said modestly.

"Indeed I do," Uncle Ned answered. "Clarence, my friend, may I ask what fate you intend for the deck of cards you are presently so fondly caressing?"

"I thought perhaps a penny game of amusement. Would you care to join me?"

"Indeed. If you would be so kind, please deal, you Son of Satan."

The Professor began to dole out the cards. Suddenly he stopped. His eyes turned toward a woman pushing her way through the crowd. She was young and fleshy with very red lips and straggling curls of an unbelievable orange. Her skirts brushed the floor but the top of her gown seemed to have slipped somewhat. It displayed a remarkable expanse of skin and the lacy edge of an undergarment.

Scanning her, the Professor pursed his lips critically. As she swept past, he pinched her.

She screeched.

A large unshaven man who smelled of horses bounced up from the next table. He towered over the Professor.

"Did you just do something to this lady?" he drawled, betraying a Texas background.

"Me? Sir! Heaven forbid!" the Professor said. He

looked aghast at being so accused.

The Texan glowered at him, then looked to the girl. She was rubbing the pinched part and frowning indignantly. The Texan asked her, "Did he hurt you, ma'am?"

"I'll say! I expect I'll be black and blue for a week." Her voice was rather loud and very shrill. "Dammitall, it's got so a decent girl can't hardly go out in public without being insulted."

"I'm exceedingly sorry, madam," the Professor said. "I was under the mistaken impression that you were employed by this establishment."

"Me? Here?" she gave a snort. "Hell, no! I don't do that kind of thing. I got me a regular man. I only just come into this place to pick up a pint for him. I wouldn't be here at all, only he's got the trots and can't come hisself. I ain't that kind of girl."

"I'm sorry," the Professor repeated.

She went on, "I'll tell you, if my man weren't ailing, he'd sure come back and bust your tailgate, Mister!"

"I'm sorry," the Professor insisted.

The Texan gave the woman an unsteady bow and said, "Allow me, ma'am."

She smiled.

The Professor tried again. "I'm *sorry!*"

The Texan grabbed him by the front of the shirt and jerked, dragging him up out of his chair. Under its spattering of freckles, the Professor's face looked ashy white. The Texan held up a large fist in front of his nose. It had very hairy fingers and craggy knuckles.

"Oh, God!" the Professor said. "Ned!"

Uncle Ned grinned lopsidedly at him. "One flaw in an otherwise sterling and impeccable character, Clarence. A flaw that I predict will be your eventual downfall."

43

The Texan drew back the fist, cocked it, and took aim.

"*Ned!*" the Professor squealed.

Uncle Ned chuckled.

"Mister," Henry heard himself say. "You leave the Professor go. He's my friend."

The Texan didn't pay a lick of attention.

Rising unsteadily, Henry leaned on the table and kicked the Texan in the shin.

With a roar, the Texan released the Professor and turned toward Henry. The Professor dropped out of sight behind the table.

The Texan glared at Henry. Lifting an open hand as if to slap, he growled, "I'll squinch you, you stinking little puke."

"Hold, sir!" Uncle Ned declaimed in his best temperance tone. Tottering to his feet, he breathed in the Texan's face. "This youth is my ward, sir! And under my protection. But dast touch a hair of his head and you shall rue the day. Harm him and you'll answer to *me!*"

"Unh?" The Texan said, squinting at Uncle Ned.

"On the field of honor, sir!" Uncle Ned added.

The Texan swung.

Uncle Ned ducked.

The Texan swung again.

As Uncle Ned twisted away, the blow glanced along the point of his cheek. He grimaced. And shoved.

Backstepping, the Texan tried to catch his balance. But something impeded him. He toppled over the Professor, who had crouched behind his legs awaiting just such an action on Uncle Ned's part.

As the Texan sprawled, Uncle Ned grabbed the bottle and started to swing it at the Texan's head. A stranger tried to snatch it out of his hand. He changed targets, smashing it against the stranger's head instead of the

44

Texan's. Two other strangers started hitting each other. The Texan blundered to his feet and threw his fist at the nearest object—an innocent bystander. And then it seemed to Henry like everybody in the place was trying to hit somebody.

A sudden tug at his pant leg startled him. Stooping, he saw the Professor peering from under the table.

"Get Ned and come on," the Professor said. "Let's get out of here."

Dutifully, Henry tapped his uncle on the shoulder. It was the wrong thing to do. Wheeling, Uncle Ned automatically swung.

His fist connected directly with Henry's jaw.

CHAPTER 7

HENRY BECAME AWARE OF WATER. HE WAS BEING held face down and ear deep in it. Choking, he began to struggle. The hand that held him released him. Popping his head up, he gasped for air. Someone pressed a cloth into his hand. He wiped at his face with it, opened his eyes, and discovered he was kneeling at a horse trough.

"Are you all right, boy?" his uncle asked.

Uncle Ned was hunkering on one side of him, and The Professor on the other. They were on a quiet side street lit only by the glow of the moon overhead.

Henry groaned.

"Duck him again?" the Professor asked.

"No!" Henry squeaked.

"No," Uncle Ned said. Rising, he looked down at Henry and announced solemnly, "If you want to go back to the hotel I'll find a cab and pay your fare. However, you'll go alone. I do not intend to abbreviate the pleasures of my evening just to take you home."

"I'm all right," Henry managed to say. His face hurt. As he got himself onto his feet, the world swayed around him.

"Sir?" he said.

"Yes, my boy?"

"What happened?"

"A miscalculation. Never, I repeat, *never* under any circumstances, tap a man on the back in the midst of a melee such as that."

"He mistook your meaning and landed you a good one," the Professor said. He was still squatting, holding his right hand in the horse trough.

"Fisticuffs are suitable strictly as a spectator sport," Uncle Ned grumbled. "No fit occupation for a gentleman."

"You can say that again." The Professor took his hand out of the water. Cradling it with the other hand, he stood up.

"Are you hurt, sir?" Henry asked him.

"I am most sorely wounded."

"Somebody stepped on him while he was hiding under the table," Uncle Ned said. He turned to the Professor. "I trust your wounds are not too sore to permit you to continue?"

"Never!"

"And you, boy?"

"I'd like to come, sir."

"Come along, then."

"Just a minute," the Professor said. "Henry, you've got my kerchief there. Will you bind up my poor injury with it?"

The cloth Henry held was a large square of white linen. He started to wrap it around the Professor's outheld hand.

There were dark stains on the Professor's knuckles.

"Uncle Ned!" Henry said. "He's bleeding!"

"Indeed?" Uncle Ned bent to look closely at the hand. "Clarence, you are indeed injured. Why didn't you say so? I hope nothing's broken. Does it hurt?"

"Very much."

"Here, give me that." Uncle Ned took the kerchief from Henry. Gently, he bound it around the Professor's hand. "Come along, my friend, we must find you succor."

"Spirits might alleviate the pain," the Professor suggested.

"Indeed," Uncle Ned agreed.

The place they hurried to was a lot like the last, except this was even smaller. The noise was harsher, the smoke thicker, and the stockyard stench stronger. There was no music at all.

The bartender was a woman. A big one. As she stepped up to ask their orders, she jiggled all over.

The Professor grinned, his pain forgotten.

"Well, gents, you look like you've been into it," she said heartily.

She was right about that. Henry was sopping wet from the neck up, Uncle Ned's cheek had begun to discolor, and the Professor had lost his hat and collar.

Carefully, as if it were quite painful to him, the Professor rested his bandaged hand on the bar. He said, "A small set-to. A matter of a lady's honor. I fear there is an uncouth element in Omaha these days. Perhaps you would have something with which I might wash this wound?"

The bartendress seemed duly impressed. "Looks like you give the bastard a good one, Buster. Bust any knuckes?"

"I sincerely hope not." With his left hand, he picked

47

awkwardly at the bandage.

"Here. I'll do that." She pushed his hand away and started to open the knot.

"Ah, me," Uncle Ned sighed. Rather loudly, he said, "Madam, before you betake yourself to tend my unfortunate associate, will you be so kind as to let me have a bottle and a brace of glasses?"

"Huh?"

"One quart and two glasses."

"Oh. Yeah. Sure." She set them up, then returned her attention to the Professor. The two of them sidled slowly away from Henry and Uncle Ned. They spoke so softly with their heads so close together that Henry couldn't hear a word they said.

Uncle Ned poured. After a few rounds, he stopped bothering with the glasses and drank directly from the bottle. For a while, he'd swig, pass the bottle to Henry, then take it back and swig again. Eventually, he forgot about passing it to Henry.

Henry didn't mind. He was happy. Drowsy. He seated himself on the floor and leaned back against the bar. Through half-closed eyes, he gazed on an assortment of legs.

There were card games going on at several tables. Uncle Ned kept glancing at them. Each glance took longer than the one before. Bottle in hand, he drifted closer. He hove to beside one game and looked on a while. When a player dropped out, he was invited to sit in. He sat.

Henry saw his uncle put money on the table, accept some cards, put more money on the table, throw away some cards, then put more money on the table. After a while another man took all the money.

Then they did it again, with a different man taking all

48

the money. They went on that way, over and over again. It seemed a very curious game. Henry thought he'd ask the Professor about it. But when he looked up, the Professor was gone. And so was the lady bartender. A dour-faced old man with three strands of hair brushed across his bald spot had taken her place.

At the table, Uncle Ned stopped putting down money. He took a bit of paper and a pencil stub from his coat pocket. As he started to write, one of the other men made an objection. Uncle Ned answered him loudly but unintelligibly. The other man said, "Put up or get out."

Uncle Ned scowled, started to speak, then went pale. The pencil slipped from his fingers. He made a move as if to rise, then slowly slid under the table. At that, the remaining players resumed their game.

On his hands and knees, Henry crept over to look for his uncle. He found him lying there flat on his back, very still, like maybe he was sick. Or dead.

Startled at the thought, Henry backed from under the table, hauled himself onto his feet, and staggered to the bar. Leaning against it for support, he called, "Professor!"

The barkeep answered, "I don't make them fancy drinks. In here, it's whiskey, beer, or nothing."

"No," Henry explained thickly. "I—uh—the Professor—he was here—with the lady—where—now?"

"How the hell should I know? Hey, you mean that red-headed feller with the skint fingers?"

"Uh huh."

"Dolly tooken him in back. Reckon he's still in there."

"Where?" Henry asked, glancing around.

The barkeep aimed a finger at an open door in the far wall. "See that there hall? Door inside it on your left. Likely your red-headed Romeo's busy behind it."

"Thank you, sir," Henry slurred.

Chuckling to himself, the barkeep watched Henry work his way across the room to the hall.

Henry found the door. It was closed. He gave it a shove. It was latched. He puzzled about that for a moment, then knocked. There was no answer. He knocked again. Still no answer.

A terrible sense of loneliness swept over Henry. In a tone somewhat like that of an orphaned calf, he bawled, "Professor! Please, Mister Professor, sir! Are you in there?"

The Professor's voice came through the closed door. "What the gaddamned hell do you want?"

"It's Uncle Ned, Professor. Please!"

"What about him?"

"I think he's dead."

"What?"

"Dead!" Henry wailed. "Please, Professor!"

"Oh hell! Just a minute. So help me . . ."

The minute seemed an extremely long one. At last the latch clicked and the door inched open. The Professor edged out. He was in his shirtsleeves. Confronting Henry, he asked, "Just what is all this screaming about?"

"Uncle Ned's lying under the table in there and I think he's dead."

"Not likely." The Professor gave a disgusted sigh. "Come on and we'll see."

Henry led him to the table where the men were still engrossed in their game. Squatting, the Professor looked under it. He grunted and took hold of Uncle Ned's ankles. With a tug, he dragged Uncle Ned out into the light.

"Roostered," he pronounced.

"Sir?"

50

"Stone cold sluiced," he explained. "Your uncle isn't dead, Henry, but come morning he'll probably wish he were."

"Is he sick?"

"He will be."

"Maybe we ought to get him home."

"Ungh." The Professor looked over his shoulder at the hallway. He sighed deeply, then told the body on the floor, "I do not intend to abbreviate the pleasures of my evening just to carry you home to bed."

"Sir," Henry said. "*Please,* sir."

With a nod toward the game in progress, the Professor asked, "Was Ned playing?"

Henry nodded.

"Maybe he passed out in time," the Professor said hopefully. "Turn out his pockets."

"No luck," one of the players grunted without so much as looking up from his hand.

With a touch of indignity, the Professor addressed the man who'd spoken. "It is customary to at least leave a gentleman cab fare."

Still without glancing up, the gambler flipped a coin toward the Professor. He caught it on the wing.

"That's a half eagle!" Henry said.

"Yes." The Professor peered closely at it. "It's Ned's brass one."

Pocketing the coin, he asked Henry, "Do you happen to have any available funds?"

"I got eight cents."

"Ungh. Oh well. Come on, you take the bottom. I'll take the top. We'll get him home somehow."

"Yes, sir." Henry took Uncle Ned by the ankles. The Professor grabbed him under the arms. As they lifted, Uncle Ned began to snore. Together, they carried him out.

CHAPTER 8

HENRY WOKE SICK. HE HUNG HIS HEAD OVER THE EDGE of the bed and located the chamber pot just in time. Then he slept again. It was around noon before he woke feeling well enough to get up. He slaked his thirst from the pitcher on the commode, dressed, and took out the chamber pot to empty it.

When he got back he found Uncle Ned clad only in drawers, sitting on the bed with his face slumped into his hands.

As Henry walked into the room, Uncle Ned moaned and muttered through his fingers, "Stop that stomping, boy."

"Yes, sir."

"And don't shout."

On tiptoe, Henry started across the room to replace the chamber pot.

"I said stop that stomping," Uncle Ned growled.

Henry froze where he was.

Slowly Uncle Ned lifted his head. He squinted at Henry through gummy red eyes. "Slattery's," he said. "In my bag. Hand it to me."

"Yes, sir," Henry whispered. Cautiously he made his way to his uncle's traveling case. Uncle Ned winced at the sound of each step. He winced again when Henry set the chamber pot on the floor. And again when Henry clicked open the case.

Henry held out the bottle.

"Open it," Uncle Ned groaned.

Henry pulled the cork. It made a sharp pop. Uncle Ned flinched and shuddered. Reaching out a trembling hand, he clutched the bottle. With both hands, he steered it to his lips. The act of swallowing seemed painful to him. Staunchly, he emptied the bottle.

"Uncle Ned . . . ?"

"Quiet, I said."

"Yes, sir," Henry mumbled. He stood still, waiting.

Eventually Uncle Ned got himself onto his feet. He finished the water in the pitcher. Very slowly and stiffly, he dressed himself, then went through his pockets. He sighed as he came up emptyhanded. At last, he turned to Henry and spoke.

In a hoarse, limp voice, he said, "I was gambling last night?"

"Yes, sir."

"Have *you* any money, boy?"

"Eight cents."

"Not so loud."

"Eight cents," Henry repeated in a whisper.

Uncle Ned muttered, "I *had* over two thousand dollars."

"Sir?"

In reply, Uncle Ned simply sighed deeply, then said, "Come on along, boy. Quietly."

Slowly, and rather unsteadily, Uncle Ned led Henry through the streets of Omaha to the lot where the Professor's wagon was parked.

The tailgate was latched shut. Uncle Ned knocked gently at it.

"Hullo?" The Professor's cheery voice came from inside. "Somebody at the door?"

"It is I," Uncle Ned moaned.

"Come on around to the front."

Bracing a hand against the wagon, Uncle Ned moved down its length. With a lot of effort and some help from Henry, he got himself up into the driver's seat.

A curtain hung between the bench seat and the body of the wagon. The Professor was holding it open, peering out.

He grinned and said, "Good morning, Ned. How are you this lovely morning? Bright and chipper as usual, I presume?"

Ned made a noise through his nose, then said, "Do you always revel so in the suffering of others, Clarence?"

"I do when they force me to abbreviate the pleasures of my evening just to carry them home to bed. Especially when they persist in calling me Clarence."

"You have no soul."

"No? Must have misplaced it. Oh well, it was pretty thin and ragged anyway."

"And now you haven't even the decency to invite a poor agonized fellow creature in for a cup of coffee."

"How thoughtless of me! Dear old Ned, how good of you to call! Please do come in and have a cup of coffee!"

"Delighted, my boy, delighted. How kind of you to ask," Uncle Ned answered weakly. He gave the Professor a feeble smile as he accepted the proferred hand and crawled over the back of the wagon seat.

The Professor's bunk was piled with rumpled bedding. Pushing aside a pillow, Uncle Ned lowered himself gently to a sitting position. Henry went to perch quietly on the box in the corner.

"Henry, you're looking well, all considered. How do you feel?" the Professor asked as he fired up his camp stove.

"I *was* tolerable sick, but I'm all right now. Except I got kinda a sore jaw and a awful thirst."

"Oh, the enviable recuperative powers of youth," Uncle Ned muttered.

"Coffee won't take long," the Professor said. Filling the pot with water, he set it on the stove.

Uncle Ned suggested, "You might put in some fresh grounds."

"Why? I've only used these four or five times."

"Fresh grounds do wonders for the flavor."

"How about a wooden nutmeg?"

"Not the same thing at all."

"Oh well." The Professor took a handful of beans from a cannister. Looking at them, he said, "These damned things have gotten precious expensive."

"Would you put a price on succor to your fellow man?" Uncle Ned said.

"Would you pay?"

"No."

"I thought not." The Professor dumped the beans in his coffee mill and began to grind them.

"How's your hand, Professor?" Henry asked.

"It will heal, I suppose. No thanks to your uncle."

"What have *I* to do with it?" Uncle Ned grunted.

"I was just proceeding into a most salubrious treatment from a very charming and abundant nurse last night when I was rudely interrupted. To attend *your* needs, Ned. Believe me, I had absolutely *no* desire to abbreviate such a promisingly pleasurable evening just to carry *you* home to bed."

Uncle Ned winced. "That explains your surly attitude this morning. Your ungodly enjoyment of my suffering."

"Vengeance is sweet," the Professor allowed.

Uncle Ned answered, "Revenge is the poor delight of little minds."

"Seneca?"

"Juvenal. How's the coffee coming?"

"He that drinks fast, pays slow, eh Ned?" The Professor took a cloth from under the stove, dampened it and offered it to Uncle Ned.

"Poor Richard?" Uncle Ned said, accepting the cloth. He pressed it to his forehead.

The Professor nodded. He set up cups, then checked the coffee pot. Uncle Ned looked hopefully at him. He answered the look. "Not yet. By the way, Ned, I note a bluish blush upon Damask cheek. How will that look to your temperance audiences?"

Uncle Ned touched a fingertip to the bruise under his eye. He sighed deeply. "Perhaps I should have it leeched."

"Leeches are horrid things. I may have something—" The Professor squatted to dig into a cabinet. He came up with a small jar.

"A lady left this," he told Uncle Ned as he uncapped the jar. It contained a flesh-colored salve. "Most useful for certain applications. Women use it to delude us as to the imperfections of their complexions."

"Thank you, old friend," Uncle Ned said, taking the jar. "How's the coffee coming?"

The Professor checked again. He nodded, picked up the pot, and poured each cup about half full. He filled them up at the keg of corn singlings.

Uncle Ned reached eagerly for a cup. Holding it in both hands, he drank deeply and sighed with pleasure. Smiling slightly, he said, "It was quite an evening, eh, Clarence?"

"Ned, please."

"Sorry, my friend."

Henry tasted his own drink. The coffee was very bitter, but the whiskey dominated it.

"Clar—er—Professor," Uncle Ned said. "I fear I find my present circumstances rather—uh—"

56

"No."

"Eh?"

"Even were I willing, I could by no means lend you money, Ned, old friend."

"What leads you to believe I wish to avail myself of your financial assistance?"

"Don't grift me. I was there. I know your weakness." The Professor turned toward Henry. "Your Uncle Ned has a fatal flaw in an otherwise sterling and impeccable character, you know."

"Sir?"

Uncle Ned answered, "When in my cups, my boy, I fear I have a slight tendency to flirt with Dame Fortune, to my own misfortune."

"He gambles," the Professor explained. "And loses."

"Loses?"

"Always," Uncle Ned admitted. He looked at the Professor. "But I have a plan."

"Of course."

"I have a mark on the hook."

The Professor showed interest. "That Philadelphian?"

Uncle Ned nodded. "However it requires a capital investment."

"Even if I were willing," the Professor said. "I couldn't. My resources are nil."

Uncle Ned glanced significantly around the room. "Knowing you, I find it difficult to believe that every nook and cranny of this cozy rolling home of yours isn't stuffed to overflowing with coin of the realm."

A sadness came into the Professor's eyes. "It was. But when the charming Judith deserted me in Julesburg, she cleaned me out. Every last cent I had hidden on the premises."

"Poor Clarence," Uncle Ned said sympathetically.

57

But then with a bit of a smirk, he added, "A fatal flaw, my friend."

The Professor sighed.

"But that was in Julesburg," Uncle Ned continued. "I trust business has been satisfactory since then."

"I've managed to victual myself."

"And put a bit aside?"

"I swear it, Ned. I've saved only a mere pittance."

"How mere?"

"Hardly more than four hundred."

"Four hundred might suffice."

"And you're not getting your greedy hands on a cent of it."

Uncle Ned looked indignant. "I *meant* to offer you a business proposition. A *profitable* business proposition."

"Profitable?"

"A ten percent return on a few hours investment."

Now it was the Professor's turn to look indignant. "You ask me to risk my entire life's savings, the security of my old age, for a paltry ten percent?"

"There is absolutely no risk involved."

"There is always the risk of my never laying eyes on you—or my money—again."

"You have my solemn oath, my friend."

The Professor stepped over to the keg and drew a little more whiskey into his coffee. Thoughtfully, he said, "Tell me the scheme."

"And have you move in to cut me out?"

"Sirrah! You impugn my honor!"

"What honor?" Uncle Ned said. He held out his cup. "Would you be so kind as to replenish this, my friend?"

"Certainly." The Professor took the cup and filled it. As he handed it back, he added, "Mine honor is my life; both grow in one; take honor from me and my life is done."

"Honor and profit lie not in one sack," Uncle Ned quoted back at him.

He answered, "Without money honor is nothing but a malady."

"Racine," Uncle Ned said. "Look, Clarence, let us cease this rhetoric and bare the bones of the matter. At the moment, you are in uncomfortable straits and I am in intolerable ones. You have some capital and I have a con. We can pool our resources to the benefit of us both. As sincere disciples of Mammon, let us reach an amicable agreement and get on with the business."

"How much do you expect to take him for?"

"I anticipate doubling the investment."

"Eight hundred. That's not much."

"You haven't much capital for me to work with."

The Professor sucked breath between his teeth. He suggested, "I supply the nut and you take the simp and we cut the butter down the middle."

Uncle Ned shook his head.

Henry looked from one to the other, wondering what they were talking about.

"I shan't dilly-dally," Uncle Ned said. "Ten percent is a more than fair return on your investment, but in view of our mutual situation, I'll up the ante to twenty percent."

"Make it thirty."

"That's hardly a generous attitude."

"I have not one single generous fiber in my entire being, Ned, and you know it."

Uncle Ned nodded. Painfully, he allowed, "Twenty-five percent. A hundred dollars, Clarence, just for the use of your four hundred, just for a few hours. If you won't go for that, then forget it. I'll find some other banker."

"Not likely."

"Then I'll find myself a con that doesn't call for capitalization." Rising, he refilled his own cup.

The Professor frowned throughfully off into the distance.

Holding out his cup, Henry asked, "Can I have some more, Uncle Ned?"

"Huh? Oh. Yes, of course. Help yourself, my boy."

He helped himself to the coffee and added a healthy dollop of the whiskey.

"You seem to be developing a taste for the finer things," Uncle Ned commented.

"Sir?"

"Strong spirits."

"Yes, sir," Henry admitted. He sipped and said, "It is right nice stuff, sir. Taken in moderation, like you said. What's a con, Uncle Ned?"

"A business deal involving the separation of a sucker from his bundle."

"It's not anything evil, is it?"

"Would you suspect your old Uncle Ned of anything evil?"

"No, sir."

"Good lad." Uncle Ned turned to the Professor. "What about it, Clarence? Twenty-five percent. A hundred dollars. Cash. For nothing."

"If you call me Clarence again, sirrah, you shall never again have from me so much as one drop of my coffee, not to mention my medicinal spirits."

"Then you'll do it!"

"Grudgingly."

"Good lad!" Uncle Ned clapped him on the shoulder. "Here, your cup's empty. Let me fill it again for you."

"From my own stock, of course," the Professor said.

"Of course!" Uncle Ned replied.

CHAPTER 9

BACK AT THE HOTEL ROOM, UNCLE NED STRIPPED TO his drawers and thoroughly bathed all his exposed parts. As he was dressing again, Henry asked him, "Uncle Ned, sir, what was that word?"

"What word?"

"The one about taking somebody's money away from him."

"Ah yes. Con," he replied. "Con, my boy. A word to be held in trust, never exhibited but before one's intimates. In other words, don't use it in public."

"Yes, sir. Sir?"

"Yes?"

"You wouldn't con the Professor, would you, sir?"

"Why, what on earth ever put such a bizarre notion into your young head?"

"I dunno. I just kinda—uh—uh—"

"My boy, as a man of honor, I would *never* in *any* situation con a friend. Except, of course, in dire necessity or otherwise extenuating circumstances. Now, give me that eight cents you mentioned."

"Sir?"

"I have exactly twenty gold eagles from Clarence. I shall need small change for operating expenses as well. Give me the eight cents." Uncle Ned smiled as he held out his hand. "You shall have it back. I promise."

Henry fished the coins from his pocket. A five cent piece and three pennies. As he gave them up, he asked, "Will I get a profit, like you promised the Professor?"

Uncle Ned cocked a brow at him. "Would you con your own uncle, my boy?"

"No, sir. Only I thought—er—"

"Ah me!" Uncle Ned sighed. He smiled again. "You're learning, boy. Abominably slowly, perhaps, but learning. You shall have your profit. Now, I have a part for you in this venture. Listen closely and be certain you understand your instructions."

"Yes, sir."

While he tied his cravat and then daubed a bit of flesh-colored makeup over his bruised cheek, Uncle Ned described the impending operation. He went over it in detail, making Henry repeat his part again and again. And again, until he was convinced that Henry actually understood. Finally satisfied with his own appearance and Henry's grasp of the plan, he led the way toward the stockyards.

Behind high fences, cattle bawled, pigs squealed, sheep bleated, goats baaahed, horses whinnied, and all stank. Men on horseback rode among the milling animals while men on foot peered through the fence rails at them.

Per instructions, Henry waited at the corner of a building across the street while his uncle located a cattleman named Slaughter. Uncle Ned talked at some length with Mister Slaughter, all the time studying the cattle bunched up in one pen. Then, at last, he took off his hat and wiped his brow.

That was Henry's cue.

Clutching the note Uncle Ned had prepared back at the hotel, and mentally practicing his speech, he trotted across the street. He pulled up in front of his uncle and opened his mouth. Nothing came out. His mind had suddenly gone completely blank.

"What is it, boy?" Uncle Ned said.

"Uh," Henry answered.

Uncle Ned prompted, "Are you perchance seeking someone in particular?"

Then it came back. All in a rush, the words spilled out of Henry just the way he'd rehearsed them. "Excuse me, sir, but I convey a message addressed to a Mister Edward Oldcastle. Would you perchance be acquainted with that goodly gentleman?"

"I am indeed he."

Henry held out the note. Uncle Ned took it and gave him a five cent piece in return. Henry pocketed the money and stood there.

"You may go now," Uncle Ned told him.

"Uh—er—yes, sir." Obediently Henry trotted back to the corner across the street and hid himself behind the building.

Uncle Ned opened the note. He frowned as he scanned it.

"I hope it ain't bad news," Slaughter said.

"For me, sir, but perhaps not for you," Uncle Ned answered. "It is from my employer. Circumstances require that the beef he desires be shipped with the utmost dispatch. He asks if it is at all possible to get at least one carload on the rails today."

"I reckon it can be done," Slaughter allowed. "If we agree on a price, I could get the critters in the pen here onto the cars today. Get the rest in and loaded first thing Monday. *If* we agree on a price."

Uncle Ned glanced at the cattle in the pen. "You warrant the entire herd is of as sound quality as these specimens?"

"I do, sir. Prime beef, every one of 'em," Slaughter said.

"Oh, would that I had the time to examine the entire lot," Uncle Ned mumbled. He licked his lips thoughtfully as he stared at the penned animals. He said, "Not one red cent more than four thousand for the lot."

Unbridled joy flickered across Slaughter's face. At best he'd hoped for thirty five hundred. He would have settled for three thousand. Suppressing his jubilation, he looked intently at Uncle Ned and suggested tentatively. "They're easy worth five thousand."

"Nay, sir! Were it not imperative the shipment begin today, my offer should not be so generous as it is. However, this decision is not solely mine own, but my employer's as well. I am merely his agent. Will you, or will you not, accept my offer?"

"Four thousand cash?"

"Oh dear!" Uncle Ned flung a hand up to his forehead.

"You got a pain?" Slaughter asked.

"This is Saturday!"

"Uh huh."

"The banks are closed."

"Oh." Slaughter's enthusiasm sagged. "You ain't got the cash in hand?"

"It is on deposit. I can have it for you first thing Monday."

"Only you want me to start shipping the critters today?" Slaughter sounded downright suspicious.

"It is imperative, Mister Slaughter. We are both men of honor. I have some pocket money on me. Suppose I give you a deposit and my own personal note for the balance?" Uncle Ned paused, gauging the depth of Slaughter's distrust against the height of his greed, then added, "I have excellent references."

"Hereabouts?"

"Of course." He reeled off the names of some of the clergymen with whom he'd arranged temperance

64

lectures for the following day.

Slaughter lit on a familiar one. "The Reverend Tucker, you say? And just how much did you have in mind to make deposit on the beef?"

"Oh, say, ten percent. In gold."

"Gold? Four hundred?"

"Yes."

"Hold on a minute." Slaughter waved one of the riders over and whispered something to him. The. rider nodded and galloped off up the street. Slaughter told Uncle Ned, "He'll be back in a minute. Care for a short one while we wait?"

"I fear not. Indulgence in alcoholic spirits is not in keeping with my personal principles."

"Oh."

"However, we could be drawing up the necessary papers for transfer of title to the herd while we await your emissary."

By the time the rider returned, the papers were ready for Slaughter's signature. The rider announced,

"Parson Tucker says Mister Oldcastle is a real respected gentleman. He's gonna speak at the church tomorrow."

Slaughter signed the papers.

Uncle Ned handed over the Professor's four hundred in gold and scrawled a promissory note for the balance. He and Slaughter shook hands. Then Slaughter headed for the nearest saloon to celebrate, while Uncle Ned ambled across the street to pick up Henry.

Assistance wasn't needed in the second phase of the operation. Uncle Ned left Henry at the hotel, then went in search of Samuel Fairweather.

The Philadelphian was pleased when Uncle Ned told him the Professor had, indeed, received spiritual guidance concerning the desired herd of cattle. He was

65

delighted when Uncle Ned admitted acting on his behalf in obtaining them. He was overwhelmed when Uncle Ned told him the price was a mere two thousand in cash for the lot. He willingly added on the five hundred that Uncle Ned suggested would be a fair reward to the Professor for his spiritual consultation.

Back at the hotel, Uncle Ned poured heaping handsful of gold coin on the bed. Seating himself, he merrily ran his fingers through them.

"That sure looks like a lot of money," Henry said, awed.

Twenty-five hundred," Uncle Ned admitted with pride.

"Sir?"

"Yes?"

"About my eight cents . . ."

Uncle Ned looked solemnly at Henry. "Boy, a person who trusts his assets to someone else without solid security, without even so much as a note of obligation, is what we call a sucker. In this world, it is the rightful due of a sucker to be conned."

"You mean me?"

"Ah—what did you say your name is?"

"Henry Caleb Lacey, Junior, sir."

"Well, Henry Caleb Lacey Junior Sir, you have all the makings in you of a first-class, A-number-one sucker. However, you are presently in the position of having an unparalleled opportunity to relieve yourself of this unfortunate affliction. Heed your wise old uncle well. Learn the lessons of life that are now so readily available to you. With study, perseverance, and luck, my boy, you may someday cast off your sad condition and walk proudly among the fraternity of grinders, grifters, and slickers."

"Yes, sir. Sir?"

"Yes?"

"About my eight cents . . ."

"As I recall, I returned five cents to you at the stockyards."

"Uh—er—I guess so. I guess I forgot."

"Indeed?" Uncle Ned lifted a brow at him. "You wouldn't try to con your old uncle, would you, boy?"

"No, sir!"

"A shame. Oh well. You'll learn." Uncle Ned dug around in a pocket and came up with three pennies. He handed them over to Henry.

"Sir?"

"Yes?"

"You promised me I could have a profit, like the Professor."

"Did I?"

"Yes, sir."

Uncle Ned produced two more pennies and held them out. "Here. And take note, boy, that it is through your kindly old uncle's generosity that you now have this cash in hand. It would have been quite simple for me to withhold it. Without a written agreement countersigned by reliable witnesses, you would have been in a poor position to press your case. To put it precisely, you could quite easily have been conned."

"Yes, sir," Henry admitted. Pocketing the pennies, he sat down. He watched Uncle Ned counting money for a moment, then asked, "Sir, what about the Professor's share?"

"Ah yes, Clarence."

"You *will* give him his money, won't you, sir?"

"Indeed, I suppose I must. There is yet another service I shall require of him." Uncle Ned began to dole coins into a separate pile. He counted out the four hundred the Professor had loaned him, then rather reluctantly added a hundred more.

Following the tally on his fingers, Henry frowned. Confused, he said, "Uncle Ned, sir, you told the Professor you were going to make four hundred dollars profit and you'd give him twenty-five percent of that. But just now you said you've got twenty-five hundred dollars there. Wouldn't that make the profit twenty-one hundred dollars, and the Professor's share—"

"Boy," Uncle Ned interrupted. "If you persist in this line of thought, if you let slip so much as one word concerning this aspect of the transaction to Clarence, I assure you, you shall rue the error of your ways."

"You are conning the Professor, ain't you, sir?"

"No more so than he would con me, had he the opportunity."

"He wouldn't really do that, would he?"

Uncle Ned smiled fondly. As if he were paying the Professor quite a friendly compliment, he said, "My boy, our friend Clarence is a grubby grabby grifting son of a whore who would happily sell me down the river, and you too, for a York shilling."

"I think he's nice," Henry said.

"I am quite nice myself," Uncle Ned answered. "And I'd do no less, should the opportunity arise. It's the way of the world, my boy, the way of the world. Now, pack your satchel. We're leaving town today."

"But your temperance lectures tomorrow—"

"I fear the fair city of Omaha must continue in its sinful ways without the enlightenment of my uplifting moral lectures. Come along, boy."

The Professor had finished his afternoon pitch. His audience had departed. He sat alone on the edge of the stage, his legs dangling. His money box was in his lap and his chin was in his hands. The customary expression of amusement that lurked in his eyes was veiled by anxiety as he gazed into the distance.

When he saw Uncle Ned and Henry round a corner he jumped down and trotted anxiously toward them.

"You pulled it off?" he asked.

Unspeaking, Uncle Ned tugged a pouch from his pocket. He jangled it, then handed it over.

The Professor hefted it, peeked inside, and sighed. Grinning, he gestured toward the wagon. "Come on in! We'll toast this joyous occasion!"

Inside, he told Henry and Uncle Ned to help themselves to refreshments. Sitting down on the bed, he poured the coins from the pouch. He ran his fingers through them, counted them and carressed them.

"You're a good man, Ned," he said.

"Have I ever let you down?" Uncle Ned said as he started to settle on the bunk.

"Not so close to the cash." The Professor waved him to the far end, then answered. "Yes."

"When?"

"Often."

"Would you ever let me down, Clarence?" Uncle Ned said.

The Professor raised a brow at him. "What do you want of me now?"

"Nothing that will cost you a cent, my friend."

"In that case, have I ever denied you a favor, Ned?"

"Yes"

"When?"

"Often," Uncle Ned replied.

"Of course," the Professor agreed. "Now, what is this service that you require of me at present?"

"Conveyance in this curious contrivance you call home."

"Yes. I should have realized as much. Did you have any particular destination in mind?"

"Any convenient railway station west of here will suffice."

"Fremont?"

"Fine."

"Is speed of the essence?"

"It is desirable but not essential. Any time today will do."

"After my evening pitch?"

"Fine."

"Agreed, then."

They shook hands on it.

"Ned," the Professor said. "There's one thing I'm extremely curious about."

"What might that be?"

"Just how much more did you take than you've admitted?"

"Come now, Clarence!"

"I do wish you wouldn't call me that."

CHAPTER 10

SPLURGING, UNCLE NED TOOK SLEEPING CAR PASSAGE from Fremont for himself and Henry. The car was a veritable palace on wheels. Brussels carpeting covered the floor. The walnut woodwork was polished to a mellow glow. The red plush seats astonished Henry by opening up into beds. There was even a washroom with all the necessaries.

The train proved terrifyingly fast. The entire trip to San Francisco took only five days. Henry spent most of the days staring out the window. Uncle Ned napped or read.

Near Potter, Nebraska, Henry saw a prairie dog village so huge that he tugged Uncle Ned's sleeve for attention, shouted and pointed.

Uncle Ned took a cursory look and commented that the village had dwindled appreciably since he'd seen it last, and he was afraid it would soon be gone altogether.

West of North Platte, Henry spotted buffalo. A whole passel of them were grazing in the distance. He was so excited at the sight that he grabbed Uncle Ned's sleeve, shouted and pointed.

Uncle Ned gave the buffalo a quick glance and said it was a paltry pack of pitiful creatures compared to the mighty herds that could have been observed from this very train only a few years earlier.

Approaching Ogalalla, Henry saw a young Indian on a spotted pony galloping across the plain. Thrilled, he grabbed Uncle Ned's sleeve, shouted and pointed.

Uncle Ned sighed and told him how only a few years ago a passenger on this line might have seen entire tribes on the move, or even a hunting party or a war party in full feathers and paint.

When the train struggled up Sherman Summit and wound its way through the awful grandeur of the Rocky Mountains, Henry didn't say a thing. He was afraid the mountains might have shrunk considerably in the past few years.

Once they crossed the line into California, Uncle Ned put away his book and indulged himself in a few fond

71

reminiscences. He reveled especially in his recollections of an area of San Francisco he called Sydney-town. Henry didn't understand much of what he said, but from the tone of his voice and the sparkle in his eyes, Sydney-town seemed a most marvelous place.

At last the conductor announced their imminent arrival in San Francisco. As the train pulled into the station, Henry stood ready. The instant the door opened, he hustled out, luggage in hand.

Outside the station, Uncle Ned hailed a cab. Ensconced in it, Henry peered through an isinglass window at the city of San Francisco.

Back in Omaha, he had thought he was seeing the elephant. He hadn't imagined then that there could possibly be a grander city than that. But San Francisco was to Omaha as Omaha had been to Serenity.

It was beyond description.

The cab clattered along the crowded streets, winding up and down and in and out and around and around until he lost all sense of direction. He didn't care. He just gaped at the sights he passed.

They left the commercial center for a residential district. The houses perching precariously on the slopes were all small and built of wood, and no two seemed painted the same color. On the high side of the street, long staircases wound up through flower gardens to front doors. On the low side, they wound down.

The cab halted in front of a yellow two-story house with bay windows jutting from the upper floor. White-painted steamboat gingerbread ornamented the eaves. A fanlight with ruby colored panes was set over the door. Geraniums and fuchsias grew in the yard.

Henry unloaded the luggage while Uncle Ned matched the cab driver for the fare. Uncle Ned lost.

Cheerily, he paid up and headed toward the house. Lugging the luggage, Henry followed him up the long flight of wooden steps to the stoop.

There was a curious little handle in the door. Uncle Ned twisted it and a bell jangled inside. After a moment the door opened. The woman who answered it was black and buxom and sleepy-eyed. For the time it took to draw a long breath, she just stared at Uncle Ned. Then, flinging her arms around his neck, she shouted, "Ned! You damned old dog!"

Uncle Ned caught her by the waist and lifted, hefting her an inch or so off the floor. Smiling, he said, "Nell, my dear, it's been a long time."

He let her down then, and she stepped back to look him over. "Too long, you double-dealing flukum juicer. Where the devil have you been all these years?"

"Everywhere. Aren't you going to invite me in?"

"Come on in!"

Henry followed them into a small entryway. To the left an arch opened into a parlor. Straight ahead lay a narrow hall and a staircase.

"All right, boy," Nell said. "You can put the bags down here."

He put the bags down.

Nell looked at Uncle Ned. "Well?"

"Well?" Uncle Ned asked.

"Not broke again?" she said with a sigh.

"By no means."

"Then tip the boy and send him on his way."

"Oh! Oh, no, my dear, the boy's not a hired lackey. He's with me."

"With you?" She widened her eyes at him. "Ned, don't tell me you've changed your style! You never struck me as the type. Fair female hearts will be

73

shattered from the great Atlantic to the broad Pacific."

"Heavens, no!" he protested. "Nothing like that at all, as I'll be delighted to demonstrate at the soonest opportunity. No, indeed, the boy's merely my nephew."

Nell looked closely at Henry. "That explains some small family resemblance, but not his presence here."

"I inherited him."

"Has he a name?"

Uncle Ned turned to Henry. "What did you say your name was, boy?"

"Henry Caleb Lacey, Junior, sir."

"Nellie, Henry. Henry, Madame Nellie Festus."

"Ma'am," Henry said respectfully.

"Charmed." Madame Nellie held the back of her hand toward him.

He took the hand and shook it vigorously.

"No!" Uncle Ned groaned. "A gentleman does not handle a lady as if she were a water pump. Watch me, my boy."

Demonstrating, he took Nellie's hand gently in his. He lifted it, bowed slightly, and pressed his lips to her knuckes.

Nellie grinned. She told Uncle Ned, "Make yourself at home in the parlor. I've got tea cooking in the kitchen."

"What, no serving wench? Don't tell me you are in financial straits, Nell, my dear?"

"It's the maid's day off," she answered, turning toward the kitchen.

"Excellent," Uncle Ned muttered. He gestured for Henry to come along into the parlor.

It was a cheery room furnished with deep-cushioned club chairs and love seats. There was a taboret and a china cuspidor convenient to each chair. A tall parlor organ graced one corner. Chromos of bowls of fruit and dead fowl ornamented the walls.

Uncle Ned sat down on a love seat and motioned Henry to a chair. Nellie came back with a tray holding a teapot, cups and a full brandy decanter. As she poured, Uncle Ned asked her, "Where are the girls?"

"I don't keep girls any more." She handed him a cup of half tea, half brandy.

"Don't tell me you've retired from business?"

"Goodness, no. I've just changed my line." She handed a cup to Henry, then poured for herself. "I run a nice discreet place where a respectable gentleman or lady can bring a companion for a small libation and a little privacy. By appointment only."

"Ah!" Uncle Ned sounded impressed. "Wonderful! Congratulations, my girl. I always knew you'd rise in the world. Even in those far bygone days when you were working out of that cowyard on Dupont Street, you had something the other girls lacked."

"Yeah," Nellie agreed. "A regular bath. Have another?"

"Don't mind if I do." He held out his empty cup. As she filled it, he asked. "How are things in Sydney-town these days?"

"Terrible. The new gangs, they call them Hoodlums, are giving the poor Chinese hell. Some time ago, they went on a rampage. Set fire to all the laundries and assaulted every yellow whore they could lay hands on. It took the National Guard and a Committee of Safety to cool the town down again."

Henry suddenly spoke. "Uncle Ned, sir? What's a whore?"

"What?" Uncle Ned frowned at him.

"A whore, sir. I recollect you said the Professor was the son of one."

Nellie rolled her eyes toward Henry. "Is he real?"

Uncle Ned nodded sadly. He told Henry, "Some day I shall explain it to you in gratifying detail. However, for the moment, I have more pressing matters at hand. Nell, I trust there is room for me to domicile briefly somewhere in this edifice?"

She smiled at him. "My room?"

"I was hoping you'd say that. And the boy? Perhaps a cot in the cellar?"

"If you say so."

Uncle Ned turned to Henry again. "Boy, kindly take my traveling case upstairs."

"The last door at the end of the hall," Nellie added.

Henry went into the entryway. As he picked up the bag, he heard Nellie asking Uncle Ned, "What's wrong with him?"

He realized the *him* she meant was him. Hesitating, he listened.

"An exceedingly deprived childhood," Uncle Ned explained. "Abysmally ignorant. And not the brightest lad in the world, I fear."

"Just how deprived can a boy that age be?"

"You wouldn't believe it, Nellie. Actually there's rather a sad tale behind it. My sister, Olivia, poor creature, suffered an incident in her childhood that distorted her outlook beyond all imagining."

"Raped?"

"Heavens, no! Actually, she witnessed something nasty in the woodshed . . ."

"Ah."

" . . . between the house cat and the barn cat."

"Oh?"

"The house cat was a delicate ball of white fluff that baby Olivia loved dearly. The barn cat was a raucous healthy tawny Tom. Well, you know how a she-cat is. Little Olivia, hearing this ghastly screeching in the woodshed, supposed bloody mayhem was being committed. She looked in and discovered her darling bit of fluff struggling against old Tom's advances as if the creature actually resented his amorous inclinations."

"Pussy cats are just like tony pussy," Nellie observed. "The more they love it, the worse they fight it."

"Indeed," Uncle Ned agreed. "But poor Olivia never understood that. What with the memory of little Fluff's screaming struggles and the misguided moral lecturing of our dear departed mother, Olivia developed a most unnatural attitude toward nature."

"She *did* manage to produce young Henry though," Nellie said in a questioning tone.

"That, too, is a sad story. Olivia grew to her womanhood spurning all suitors. In fact she was well on the way to unrelieved spinsterhood when the senior Lacey happened along. Our dear father was fearful of having Olivia on his hands for the rest of his life, so he rather impelled her into the union. As I understand it, she dutifully allowed the consummation of the marriage, but after that one night she absolutely forbad Lacey ever to lay a hand on her again. I also understand that the experience was so unsatisfactory he willingly agreed."

"A lot of my customers have similiar domestic problems," Nellie said. "More tea?"

"Don't mind if I do."

"Tell me, Ned, what have you been doing with yourself? Not in jail, I hope."

"Thank God, no," Uncle Ned answered.

Concluding that they'd finished talking about *him*,

77

Henry carried the traveling case on upstairs. All the way up, and all the way down again, he pondered the story he'd overheard. He couldn't make sense of it at all.

CHAPTER 11

CALLERS WERE EXPECTED AT MADAME NELLIE'S THAT evening. Uncle Ned explained to Henry that the visitors would want complete privacy, handed him a fistful of little yellow-covered books and a lamp, and sent him to the cellar.

The next morning after breakfast Uncle Ned and Madame Nellie went off somewhere together. Before they left, Madame Nellie advised Henry not to wander from the house.

Henry was alone, except for the maid, a pale scrawny woman with such a nasal New England intonation that he found her totally unintelligible. He spent most of the day on his cot in the cellar reading.

It was rather a pleasant cellar, as cellars go. Two walls were dug into the side of the hill, but the other two, on the downslope, were almost entirely above ground. One had a window in it. The other had a door opening into the side yard. Heeding Madame Nellie's admonition, Henry didn't venture into the yard, but when his eyes began to ache he rested them by gazing out the window at the roof of the next house over.

That evening more callers who wanted privacy were expected, so Henry lit his lamp again and lolled about the cellar reading until he fell asleep. The next morning, Uncle Ned and Madame Nellie went out again.

The following day was much the same.

And the day after that.

For a while, Henry was satisfied. The books were unlike anything he'd ever encountered before. He'd never even dreamed of such thunderous adventures. But by the end of a week, he was wondering when he'd actually get to *see* some fabulous sights, instead of just reading about them.

He broached the subject one morning at breakfast.

"Uncle Ned, sir?"

"Unh?" Uncle Ned said through a mouthful of shirred egg.

"Uncle Ned, sir, I'd—uh—I want to see San Francisco."

"Oh? You do, do you?"

"Yes, sir."

Madame Nellie nodded and said, "He's right, Ned. It isn't fair to leave him cooped up here all day while we're enjoying ourselves. Suppose we take him to the park this afternoon. Or we could drive out to Cliff House—"

Eagerly, Henry interrupted, "I want to see The Billy Goat, and the Bull Run, and the Opera Comique, and the Bella Union."

"Ned!" Madame Nellie exclaimed.

Uncle Ned lifted a brow at Henry.

"I want to see all of Sydney-town," Henry added.

Uncle Ned smiled at fond recollections. He turned to Madame Nellie. "It would be pleasant to visit old haunts. This evening, perhaps. Would you be free to join us, Nell?"

"Ned Oldcastle! Do you have any idea what you're proposing?" she said with a frown.

Uncle Ned looked puzzled. "An educational tour of the town for the boy."

"Have you no scruples?"

"Never had one in my life. What's wrong, my dear?"

"You want to take this sweet innocent child to the Barbary Coast?"

"Why, my dear, I had no idea you disapproved so of our old stomping grounds."

"It's not that I disapprove," Nellie said. "But it isn't the Sydney-town we used to know, Ned. The old gangs, the Ducks and Rangers, don't run the show any more. It's all Barbary Coast Hoodlums now. A bunch of young punks who'd hustle you and this poor boy the same as they would any flush slummers."

"I am quite capable of taking care of myself."

"Are you, Ned? They'd spice your drinks with sulphate of morphine and you'd find yourself stripped in some alley. Or dead. And the poor boy, most likely he'd discover himself signed onto a tea clipper bound for China."

"China?" Henry asked.

"A lot of sailors jump ship in San Francisco," Madame Nellie explained. "Outbound ships are often shorthanded. A healthy young man who passes out in a low dive is likely as not to be sold to fill an empty berth before he wakes up. And if he doesn't pass out, he's likely to be knocked on the nog by some crimp or runner and loaded on board just before a ship sails."

"I am sure you exaggerate, my dear," Uncle Ned protested.

"I want to see San Francisco," Henry muttered, his hopes waning.

Madame Nellie smiled sweetly and assured him, "You shall Henry. I promise. This afternoon, we'll go for a drive to the park."

Henry might have really enjoyed the drive, if he hadn't been preoccupied with thoughts of all the more exciting sights he was missing. But after the drive, the situation improved. They went to Carr's for dinner.

Uncle Ned described Carr's as a quiet out-of-the-way little restaurant with excellent cuisine. Henry found it a wonder comparable with the sleeping cars of the Transcontinental Railway.

The building appeared as he might have imagined the castle of some Spanish Grandee such as he'd been reading about. Every inch of it was ornamented with turrets, tall windows and turned work.

Inside, the walls were paneled with oiled walnut. The windows were draped in wine velvet with deep golden fringes and long tassels. Warm mellow light flooded from chandeliers that dripped with crystal prisms. Each table was dressed in white damask. The waiters wore red jackets with shiny brass buttons. They moved noiselessly across the thick carpeting, appearing suddenly when needed, disappearing discreetly when unwanted.

A soft-spoken waiter with a very large nose escorted Uncle Ned's party to a table, held a chair for Madame Nellie, then handed each of them a large card on which curious words were listed. Uncle Ned ordered Martini Gins for himself and Henry, and a cordial for Madame Nellie. The waiter faded away. Henry squinted at the list on the card.

"Sir," he asked Uncle Ned. "What's this thing?"

"A bill of fare. A list of dishes available in the establishment. Order whatever you will."

"Yes, sir." Henry set himself to studying the menu. He found very few words he knew. He had heard of oysters, though he'd never seen the kind that came out of the water. He knew they were a prime delicacy. And he liked seasoning. Pointing to a listing on the menu, he asked Uncle Ned, "Can I have this?"

"Oysters in season," Uncle Ned read aloud. He chuckled.

"Sir?" Henry asked.

Madame Nellie explained, "Oysters aren't in season now, Henry. This is June. You can only get oysters in months with an R in them."

"Are?"

"September, October, November, months like that."

"Oh," Henry mumbled, embarrassed. "Ma'am, would you pick something for me?"

She was pleased to do so. She ordered one of the things Henry had never heard of. It turned out to be a steak in orange sauce, with an assortment of vegetables and breads. It was delicious.

After dinner, Uncle Ned called for brandies all around, and a stogie for himself. The waiter had just delivered them when a squat man in a frock coat bounced up to the table, clapped Uncle Ned on the back, and grinned.

"Migod, if it isn't Ned Oldcastle!"

"Fishfoot!" Uncle Ned exclaimed in response. "Come, sit down, join us!"

The waiter held a chair for the newcomer, took his order for an additional brandy and stogie, then disappeared. In a moment, he was back with the drink and cigar.

Uncle Ned introduced Madame Nellie and Henry to his old friend, Fishfoot O'Neal, a pianist by trade.

Fishfoot explained that he'd given up music for management and was presently handling a young woman, a *danseuse* he called her, who was appearing at the Bella Union.

Madame Nellie wished him well, saying that she had an appointment at the house and would have to return. Uncle Ned offered to escort her, but she answered that obviously he and Fishfoot would like to spend some time together and she and Henry could get home unattended.

The last place Henry wanted to go was back to his cellar. He protested, "Please, Uncle Ned, can't I stay with you and Mister Fishfoot?"

"Ned," Madame Nellie said.

Uncle Ned looked into Henry's pleading eyes and said, "An evening out would do the boy a world of good."

"Please," Henry said.

"Perhaps a visit to the Bella Union to see Fishfoot's *danseuse,*" Uncle Ned suggested.

Madame Nellie didn't look happy about the idea. She eyed Uncle Ned. "Just the Bella Union? No low dives?"

"My dear, would I frequent a low dive?"

"You love them."

"Please," Henry repeated.

Madame Nellie insisted, "Promise me, Ned. No low dives."

"You have my word of honor," Uncle Ned said.

She sighed reluctantly, but she gave in. Uncle Ned saw her to a cab, then returned to Henry and Fishfoot.

"The Bella Union first?" he said jovially.

"Right," Fishfoot agreed. He looked curiously at Uncle Ned. "Did you mean that about staying out of low dives?"

Uncle Ned smiled. "I find it expedient, my friend, to promise a lady whatever she wishes, regardless of my actual intentions. However, in this case, I think it would be wise to stay away from the lower dives so long as we have the boy with us. We shall start at the Bella Union, then move on to a few middle-range dives."

"Right!" Fishfoot grinned.

Henry nodded solemnly. He wondered just what it was about low dives that made them so dreadful. He wished his uncle would take him to one and show him.

The Bella Union called itself a music hall. It was entered through a bar room. Uncle Ned's party stopped briefly for refreshment, then went into one of the curtained boxes that lined the walls of the little theater. They'd no sooner seated themselves than a young woman wearing very few clothes came into the box and asked if they'd care to order some champagne.

Uncle Ned asked for Martini Gins all around.

The waitress winked at him as she left. Soon she was back with the drinks. She had what seemed to Henry a very odd walk. Kind of like a duck, he thought. This time as she left she winked at Fishfoot.

On the stage, a number of men and women were doing strange things in time to music. Henry sipped his drink and settled down to watch. Almost immediately, the music stopped and the curtain rolled down.

The waitress reappeared. Uncle Ned ordered another round. As the waitress left, she winked at Henry.

The music began again and the curtain rolled up to reveal a rather chubby young woman wearing just a few red ruffles. She began to wriggle as if she had a bad itch she couldn't quite reach.

"That's my girl," Fishfoot told Uncle Ned.

"Not bad."

"I could arrange something after the show."

84

Uncle Ned sighed. "I fear not tonight. I have this callow youth in my custody."

"I'll get him something too," Fishfoot suggested.

Uncle Ned made a pensive sound. He said, "Let me think about it. I am not at all sure the boy's ready yet."

"Ready for what, sir?" Henry asked.

Fishfoot said, "You're never too young if you can get it up."

Uncle Ned sighed again. "You don't know my ward."

Just then the curtain banged down and the waitress reappeared. Uncle Ned ordered another round.

They stayed quite a while at the Bella Union. The performances on stage intrigued Henry. He couldn't make any sense of them, but something about them gave him very funny feelings.

Eventually, Uncle Ned and Fishfoot decided to move on.

"To some low dive?" Fishfoot asked thickly.

Slurring, Uncle Ned responded, "Precisely."

They walked out together as if they'd forgotten Henry. He trotted along behind them.

The streets were filled with light and music and noises and strange smells and people. All kinds and colors of people. Well-dressed men and women, and not-so-well dressed men and women, and the grubbiest nastiest looking children Henry had ever seen.

Some of the streets seemed lined entirely with saloons. Uncle Ned and Fishfoot led him into a number of them, and sometimes remembered to order drinks for him, too.

Other streets were full of little houses with low windows. Women leaned out of the windows, gesturing. Hardly any of them seemed to be wearing clothes. Henry stared at them. They winked and motioned at him.

After a lot of other stops, Uncle Ned and Fishfoot led Henry into a place that advertised itself as The Sailor's Haven. It was an ill-lit, stinking cellar that Henry was certain must be, at best, a low dive, and probably a Den of Iniquity as well. Men stood at the bar, sat at tables, and lay about on the floor.

By then, Uncle Ned and Fishfoot had given up bothering with drinking glasses. They passed a bottle back and forth, occasionally offering it to Henry, and occasionally to any convenient bystanders. In time, they settled at a table with several other men. Feeling rather tired, Henry rested his head on the table.

Dozing, he dreamed of card games and the clank of coin.

CHAPTER 12

A LONE CAB CLATTERED ALONG THE EMPTY STREET. The glow of its side lamps was muffled by the night fog. The driver half-dozed on the box.

Inside, Fishfoot O'Neal said, "Ned, it just ain't right."

"I know," Uncle Ned groaned as the cab rolled to a stop. "Would God it were otherwise."

Fishfoot nodded sagely in agreement.

Wedged between the two of them, Henry continued to snore.

Uncle Ned squinted out of the cab. Through the fog he could make out a faint reddish glow. He assumed it was the fanlight above Madame Nellie's front door. Jostling Henry, he said, "Come along, boy."

"Unh?" Henry mumbled, still dreaming.

"Fishfoot, give me a hand with him."

The two men managed to maneuver Henry out of the

cab. Uncle Ned held him up while Fishfoot paid the driver. As the cab disappeared into the fog, the two men struggled Henry's limp form up the long wooden walk. At the door, Fishfoot held the boy up while Uncle Ned searched himself for the key. Before he could locate it, the door suddenly opened.

Silhouetted against the glow of the hall lamp, Madame Nellie faced Uncle Ned. Her hands rested on her hips. Her voice was as chilly as the fog. "Well, come on in. *If* you can."

Uncle Ned drew himself up with great dignity. Carefully enunciating each word, he said, "I assure you, Madam, I am quite capable of whatever endeavor I should desire to venture."

"I suppose you've hit every low dive from Montgomery to Stockton," Madame Nellie sighed. "Let's get that poor boy into bed before you drop him."

Carrying a candle, she led the way to the cellar. Uncle Ned and Fishfoot dumped Henry onto the cot. There was a blanket lying on the floor. Taking great care not to topple over, Uncle Ned stooped and picked it up. He spread it gently over the boy.

"You two had better come into the parlor," Madame Nellie said. "I'll fix you some coffee."

Uncle Ned and Fishfoot followed her upstairs. She saw them both safely ensconced in chairs, then went to the kitchen. Once she was out of earshot, Fishfoot said, "Ned, it just ain't right."

"I know," Uncle Ned moaned. "Now, please, shut up about it!"

Madame Nellie came back. She didn't say anything. She just stood looking at Uncle Ned.

He squirmed.

She glared.

"My dear . . ." he started. The words hung there.

Fishfoot spread his mouth in what he hoped was an amiable smile.

Uncle Ned cleared his throat. He glanced around.

Madame Nellie glared at him.

"Uh—excuse me," he said, hoisting himself to his feet. He swayed a moment, then tottered off.

Madame Nellie looked at Fishfoot.

The backdoor slammed.

Fishfoot muttered, "It just ain't right."

"What ain't right?" Madame Nellie asked.

"Selling that poor dumb kid off to China."

"*What!*"

"Oh oh," Fishfoot said to himself. He wiped his mouth with his hand. But it was too late to wipe away the slip.

"You'd better tell me just what you're talking about," Madame Nellie told him. Her hands were on her hips again, and there was fire in her eyes.

Fishfoot gulped. Slowly, he said, "Ned got himself into a gambling game."

"And he lost?"

"Uh huh."

"Of course. But what's this about Henry?"

"Ned got in deep. Awful deep. He run out of cash and took to writing paper. Damned old Captain Horne. You know him?"

Madame Nellie nodded.

"Nasty old sea rat," Fishfoot continued. "Getting stuck with all that no-good paper wouldn't sit too well with him. Not at all. He'd of had Ned's hide—"

"About Henry?" Madame Nellie insisted.

"Horne was gonna sail shorthanded. He offered to tear up all the paper and put up all the cash on one hand against the boy for a sailor," Fishfoot said sadly.

Madame Nellie nodded. "And Ned lost."

Fishfoot echoed her nod. "Now Captain Horne's supposed to send a couple of men, come through the cellar door, fetch the boy out of his bed and off to the ship without anybody knows. Especially without *you* know."

"When?"

"Just before dawn. Horne's sailing on the morning tide."

"Hell."

"No business betting nobody else," Fishfoot mumbled. "No business betting nobody but himself."

"What?"

"No business betting nobody but himself," he repeated.

Madame Nellie gave a very thoughtful nod. She went back to the kitchen.

"It just ain't right," Fishfoot said to himself.

Eventually Uncle Ned returned from the outhouse. He staggered into the parlor, plopped himself into his chair, leaned back his head, and closed his eyes. After a few minutes, he heard Madame Nellie's footsteps and the clink of cups. Then he heard her say sweetly, "Wake up, Ned. Coffee's ready."

Cautiously, he opened one eye. She stood before him, holding a tray with three cups of coffee on it. He opened the other eye, then took the nearest cup.

"You have forgiven my indiscretions, my dear?" he asked.

"Hardly," she said. "But you're the man you are, Ned. There just isn't any changing that, is there?"

"My dear!" He smiled as he lifted the cup in a gesture of a toast.

Madame Nellie handed a cup to Fishfoot. Putting down the tray, she took the last coffee for herself and settled into a chair facing Uncle Ned. She looked expectantly at him.

"Delicious," he said of the coffee, though it wasn't so. In fact it was unusually bitter. But he dutifully downed it all. And then he slowly keeled over.

"Ooops," Fishfoot observed. "Soused."

"Sandbagged," Madame Nellie corrected.

He asked, "You put something in his coffee?"

She nodded. And smiled. "Mister Fishfoot," she said. "Would you please give me a hand with him?"

"Certainly, madam." Fishfoot rose unsteadily. "Where to?"

"The cellar. We will deposit dear old Ned in the cot and bring Henry up here for the rest of the night."

"But them runners is gonna be coming to the cellar to get the boy pretty soon."

"The runners will come to the cellar to get a deck hand for a ship that sails shortly after dawn. Runners aren't particular as long as the subject is physically sound. I can attest Ned is that."

"Oh?" Fishfoot thought about it as he helped her drag Uncle Ned to the stairs. He began to chuckle. The more he thought about it, the more he chuckled. By the time they reached the cellar, his chuckles had grown into galloping guffaws.

Once Uncle Ned was laid out on the cot, Madame Nellie bent and kissed him lightly on the forehead. Tenderly, she said, "Sometimes you get what you deserve in this world, you damned conniving son of a bitch."

Henry woke curled on a love seat in Madame Nellie's parlor. He couldn't recall how he'd gotten there, or how he'd gotten home, or much of anything that had happened after he and Uncle Ned and Mister Fishfoot left the Bella Union. When he started to get up, he discovered he was too sick to care.

After several long naps, he felt better. By late afternoon, he struggled to his feet and found himself alone in the house. It was the maid's day off. He retired to his cot in the cellar and read until he fell asleep again. It wasn't until breakfast the next morning that he began to suspect something might be amiss.

Instead of Uncle Ned taking the third place at the table, Mister Fishfoot O'Neal sat down there.

Henry looked at Fishfoot. He looked at Madame Nellie. He looked at the fourth chair. There was no plate set in front of it.

He asked, "Where's Uncle Ned?"

"Gone," Madame Nellie replied.

"Gone?"

She nodded. She didn't meet Henry's eyes. When he turned to Fishfoot, Fishfoot turned away.

"You mean *gone?*" Henry said.

Madame Nellie nodded again.

"Where? When's he coming back?"

"He didn't say," she said.

Fishfoot suggested, "About two years, I'd guess."

Dismayed, Henry asked, "Didn't he say anything about me?"

"No."

"Didn't he even say goodbye?"

"He just sort of disappeared," Fishfoot said.

Madame Nellie said, "You're well rid of him."

"No, ma'am," Henry answered.

"Believe me, Henry," she told him, "Ned Oldcastle is no gentleman. No fit man to be guardian to a boy like you."

"I like him," he protested.

"You're well rid of him," Madame Nellie said again, very firmly.

Henry sunk into silence. He looked at his breakfast but he didn't feel like eating any of it. After gazing at it a while, he asked to be excused from the table.

Back in his cellar, he tried reading, but the books couldn't catch his interest. He tried sleeping some more, but he just lay there thinking of Uncle Ned.

At the sound of footsteps on the stairs, he sat up, hopefully. But it was only Madame Nellie.

"Pack your satchel, Henry," she told him. "You're going home."

"Ma'am?"

"Ned said you came from some hick town in Missouri. You're going back there."

"I don't understand, ma'am."

"San Francisco is no fit place for a child like you. You're leaving on this afternoon's train for—uh—what was the name of that place? The town where you lived?"

"I didn't live in a town. I lived on a farm."

"Well, it was near some town, wasn't it?"

"Yes, ma'am. Serenity."

"Yes, that's it. You're going back to Serenity."

"Oh," Henry said, thinking of Parson Fhew and all the little Fhews. He was afraid he'd have to live with them if he went back to Serenity.

Suddenly he brightened. "Ma'am, I can't go back there. I haven't got no money for the cars."

"I'll buy your train ticket."

Dimming, he muttered, "I haven't got no money at all."

Madame Nellie turned her back and lifted her skirt, revealing a lot of thigh and a lavender garter with a tiny

92

pistol holstered on it. There was a pocket in the garter. She took a pair of double eagles from it.

Holding the coins out to Henry, she said, "Here. This should be more than enough for expense money. Put one in your pocket and the other in your satchel. Keep one hand in your pocket and the other on your satchel all the way home. You understand?"

"Yes, ma'am," Henry said sadly.

The train was just as big and just as grand as the one that had brought Henry and Uncle Ned to San Francisco, but somehow it didn't seem nearly so fine. The Sierra Nevadas were just as magnificent as they had been, but Henry hardly saw them. He rode gazing out the window at nothing in particular. Every once in a while, he snuffled slightly. It just hadn't been right of Uncle Ned to go off and leave him and not even say goodbye or anything.

The second day out, as Henry stared at nothing in particular, a spot of color caught his eye. A wagon was coming down the road that paralleled the tracks. A red and white wagon with gilt gingerbread ornaments, drawn by a team of snow white horses.

Leaning out the window, Henry waved and shouted as loud as he could. But the man at the reins of the wagon was engrossed in conversation with the young woman who rode beside him. He didn't even notice the train.

A puff of wind flung black smoke and cinders into Henry's face. His eyes clenched shut. When he got them open again, the wagon was past, disappearing in the distance.

The train sped on, bearing Henry toward Serenity.

CHAPTER 13

THE TOWN OF BUSKIN, WYOMING, WAS A LOT LIKE A lot of other towns where the train made regular meal stops. Most of the buildings that looked so fine from the cars were really little shacks hiding behind high false fronts. To Henry, it was just another place to get off, stretch his legs, stoke his stomach, then get on again.

The conductor tromped through the cars shouting, "Forty minutes! Forty minutes!"

With one hand in his pocket and the other holding his satchel, Henry joined the horde of hungry passengers rushing to get to the restaurant. He was jostled and shoved down the aisle. At the door, someone rammed him. He went sprawling out onto the platform. Somebody stepped on him. As he scrambled to his feet, he found he'd lost his satchel. Then he saw a man in a yellow vest picking it up.

"Hey!" he shouted.

Yellow-vest grinned at him and held the satchel toward him. As he reached for it, Yellow-vest stumbled against him. Apologizing profusely, the man dusted Henry off, handed him the satchel and then hurried away.

Henry headed for the restaurant.

Buskin boasted a number of saloons where one might order a sandwich or perhaps a fried steak, but Ransom's Restaurant was its only proper eating place. The proprietor, Wilson Ransom, tried to keep a quality establishment. He put clean cloths on the tables every other day, wiped the counter after particularly sloppy customers, paid a decent wage to a decent cook, and even met the exorbitant costs of having a few outland delicacies shipped in by rail. All in all, his was one of the better meal stops along the line. The food was actually edible and seldom hazardous to the health when taken in moderation.

By the time Henry got into the dining room all the seats were taken. A couple of latecomers were standing at the far end of the counter, awaiting service. He fell in next to them.

Setting down his satchel, he leaned his elbows on the counter and gazed at the menu chalked on the wall. It listed half a dozen meat dishes, several kinds of fowl, assorted sandwiches, and oysters in season. But of course it was still June and oysters weren't in season.

Thinking of San Francisco, Henry sighed. He wondered where Uncle Ned had gone to and why he'd left so suddenly without even a goodbye.

And he wondered if he'd get waited on before time for the train to leave.

Normally Ransom had a hired man wait tables during the rush and wash dishes afterward. But yesterday the hired man had run off with a girl from Miz Maggie's establishment and so far Ransom hadn't found a replacement for him.

Today, Wilson Ransom faced the mob alone.

Apron flapping, he darted from customer to customer. He reached Henry last of all. By then, there wasn't much time left. Henry ordered a quick bowl of beef stew and a sandwich. He was only halfway through the stew when the locomotive blew its first warning.

Dishes rattled and clattered as the general pace of eating increased. Henry rapidly scooped stew into his mouth. By the second warning whistle, he was almost done. Around him, customers were finishing up and starting out. Ransom stood at the door collecting from each for his meal.

Henry bolted the last of the stew, stuffed the sandwich into his pocket and reached for his satchel.

It was gone.

"Hey!" he shouted.

Nobody paid any attention to him.

He looked around. Not a sign of the satchel. Again, he said, "Hey!"

Again, he was ignored.

Not sure just what to do, he fell into the line at the door. He was the last one. When he reached Ransom, he said, "Excuse me, Mister, but my satchel's gone."

Ransom looked him in the face and said, "Beef stew and a sandwich. Two bits."

"My satchel's gone," Henry repeated.

Ransom repeated, "Two bits."

Henry fished into his pants pocket for the money. The locomotive gave its final warning call. Ransom said once more, "Two bits."

Henry gulped as he brought an empty hand out of an empty pocket. He tried the other pants pocket. Nothing. He tried the hip pockets. Nothing.

Thinly, he said, "My money's gone."

Ransom's eyes narrowed. "Are you trying to cheat me out of two bits, Buster?"

"No, sir. Only, my money's gone. And my satchel's gone," Henry answered, trying a coat pocket. Nothing.

Wilson Ransom was tired. His feet ached. He wanted to get off them, to submerge them in a basin of hot water. He was in no mood for idle conversation.

He said, "Two bits."

Henry wished desperately that Uncle Ned were there. Uncle Ned would certainly have known what to do. The

Professor would know what to do. Madame Nellie would probably know. Likely even Mister Fishfoot would know. But Henry didn't know.

He felt the other coat pocket, under the sandwich. Nothing. There was only one pocket left. The one inside his coat, where he had his train ticket. He reached into it.

"Ugh," he said as his fingers examined the lining. The train ticket was gone too.

Outside, the locomotive hissed and began to chug. Over Ransom's shoulder, Henry saw the cars lurch, then begin slowly to roll.

"Ugh," he repeated.

"You owe me two bits," Ransom said with determination.

"Sir?" Henry said.

"What?"

"I think my train's up and went and left without me."

Ransom nodded.

Henry looked at him. "What do I do now?"

Ransom sighed. He wanted to sit down. He said, "You go back into the kitchen. The cook will show you a big tub. You begin by filling it with hot water. Then you pick up all the dirty dishes lying around here. You put them in the water, and you dive for 'em until you come up with a pearl."

"Sir?"

"What you do now, boy, is work off the two bits you owe me. That's what."

With that, Ransom turned away and plopped himself into the nearest chair.

By the time Henry was done washing the dishes, it had occurred to him he had no place to sleep the night. He approached Ransom hesitantly.

"Sir, I was—uh—thinking, sir, I—I—"

"Spit it out, boy," Ransom said.

"I ain't got nowhere to go. Nowhere to sleep or eat or nothing. I was wondering—I—uh—"

"You want regular work?"

Henry nodded.

Ransom surveyed the stacks of clean dishes. He eyed the waste bin overflowing with the remains of crockery Henry had dropped. He shifted his weight from one aching foot to the other. He sighed.

At last, he said, "All right, boy, we'll give it a try. You swamp the place out, chop the wood, wash the dishes, and whatever else needs doing. I'll pay you a dollar a week, two meals a day, and you can sleep in the storeroom. But every damned dish you break will come out of your wage, you understand?"

"Yes, sir. Thank you, sir."

"Now, there's kindling to be cut."

"Yes, sir."

By nightfall, Henry was exhausted. He spread the quilts Mister Ransom had given him on the storeroom floor, stretched out and instantly began to snore.

The next day, he swept, mopped, scrubbed, washed dishes, cut wood and even helped wait tables. He didn't actually take orders, but he helped Mister Ransom carry the food in to the customers. He'd done it very well, not dropping a single thing. Later, Mister Ransom told him that if he kept at it, eventually he might work his way up to becoming a full-fledged waiter.

That night he dreamed proudly of his promising future.

But the third day didn't get off to such a good start. When Missus Grimp, who kept chickens up by the creek, came in with the day's supply of eggs, Henry dropped the basket. All but one egg went to pieces.

Disgusted, Mister Ransom smashed the sole surviving egg, then set out to locate another basketful.

Anxiously, Henry hurried on to his next chore. He hoped he could get the day's wood supply all chopped before Mister Ransom got back. But he'd barely got started when the head went flying off the ax. Straight through the storeroom window. Fortunately, the window was open.

But instead of a dull thud from within the storeroom, Henry heard a clattery crash.

He dashed inside and discovered the axhead had downed a shelf full of ketchup bottles. The storeroom looked a shambles. Hopeful that he could get the mess cleaned up before Mister Ransom got back, he started grabbing up bits of shattered glass. He slashed his thumb.

The wound was so deep that he had to tie it up with a bit of old rag to stop the bleeding. He was just pulling the knot tight with his teeth when he heard the bell on the restaurant jangle. Figuring it was Mister Ransom with the eggs, he hurried out to give a hand.

But instead of Mister Ransom, he found a clutch of women in the dining room.

Five of them were quite young and quite pretty. They chattered and giggled together. The sixth, who presided over them like a broody hen, was older. A large stately woman with an exquisite face, a mass of golden curls, and a look of weariness, as if she hadn't slept well at all.

She addressed Henry. "You're the new boy here?"

"Yes, ma'am."

"We want a table for six."

Henry swallowed hard. There weren't any tables for six. Each little square table had only one chair to a side.

He had no idea what to do.

"Those two will be fine," the woman said, pointing. "Come along now, push them together for us."

"Oh!" Enlightenment brightened Henry's face. He rushed to shove the tables together. Doing it, he pinched his thumb and barely manage to stifle a yelp of pain.

Once the tables were together, it occurred to him to arrange the chairs appropriately. While he was doing that, he remembered how the waiters at Carr's had seated customers. Holding the chair at the head of the table, he gave a slight bow toward the woman.

Graciously, she took her place.

Henry worked his way around the table, seating each woman in turn. Then he stepped back and looked proudly at them. He wished Mister Ransom were there to see how well he'd handled the situation.

The older woman looked toward him and said, "The usual."

Suddenly flustered again, he said, "Ma'am?"

"The usual," she repeated.

He gazed blankly at her.

Impatience edged her voice as she said, "Tell the cook that Miz Maggie and the girls are here and want the usual for breakfast."

"Breakfast?"

"Yes, breakfast."

Henry wished Mister Ransom were there to take over. But Mister Ransom was nowhere in sight. Uncertainly, Henry headed into the kitchen and gave the message to the cook.

The cook grumbled, "Tell her there ain't no eggs."

Reluctantly, Henry returned to the dining room and made his announcement.

"No eggs?" Miz Maggie said incredulously.

100

"No, ma'am. No eggs."

"Ridiculous."

"Yes, ma'am," Henry said. He glanced toward the door, wishing desperately that Mister Ransom would come walking in.

Miz Maggie sighed. "Well, if there aren't any eggs, I suppose we shall have breakfast without eggs."

"Ma'am?" Henry said blankly.

"Never mind," Miz Maggie said as if her scant patience had been completely exhausted. She got to her feet and strode toward the kitchen. She delivered her order directly to the cook, chatted with him a while, then returned to the table.

Henry went to the door and looked both ways down the street, hopeful he'd spot Mister Ransom. But there wasn't a sign of the restaurant owner. And then the cook was hollering for Henry.

In the kitchen, six plates of food were already loaded onto a large tray. The cook told Henry to deliver them.

With trepidation, he took the tray into the dining room. Cautiously, he set it on an empty table. Then he took a dish from it and looked at the various girls. One nodded. He set the dish in front of her.

To his own amazement, he managed to get the dishes all doled out without a spill or a drop. He was feeling quite pleased with himself again as he started back to the kitchen with the empty tray.

The door bell jangled.

At the same instant, Miz Maggie gasped, "What's this!"

Mister Ransom came hurrying into the dining room with the egg basket on his arm just as Miz Maggie lifted something on her fork from among the crisp strips of bacon Henry had set before her. She held it out toward Ransom.

101

He stepped up and peered at it. Turning to Henry, he demanded, "What the devil is this!"

Henry took a look.

The object dangling from Miz Maggie's fork was a very dirty greasy bloody piece of rag.

Henry looked at his cut thumb. It was bare.

"Disgusting," Miz Maggie said. She set down her fork and got to her feet. "Come along, girls. I'm sure no one has any appetite left after this."

She strode away from the table, with the girls following like chicks behind a hen.

"Please, Miz Maggie," Ransom began. "I'm sure—"

"I'm sure I've never seen anything so revolting," Miz Maggie interrupted. "I hate to think of what other atrocities might be occurring in your kitchen. Believe me, I'll never eat here again. And I intend to warn all my customers. Just wait until Wade hears . . ."

With that she stalked through the door with her chicks following after her.

Ransom gently set down the egg basket. He looked at Henry. "You. Go. Get out. You hear? *Never* let me see you again."

"Yes, sir," Henry gulped as he backed toward the door. Reaching it, he dashed out.

CHAPTER 14

HENRY SLEPT THAT NIGHT IN AN EMPTY CRATE BEHIND the General Mercantile. Before dawn, it rained. He woke with a sore thumb, an aching head, and a very empty belly.

He washed his face in a horse trough. Wiping the water out of his eyes, he took a long look at the town of

102

Buskin. The businesses ranked along its lone street began with a blacksmith shop and ended with a gunsmith's. He plodded up to the gunsmith's. He stood a while, looking at the shop. Then he went in and asked for a job.

The gunsmith very pleasantly told him no.

He worked his way along the line, stopping and inquiring in each place of business except, of course, Ransom's Restaurant. He passed the restaurant hurriedly, with his head ducked and his breath held. But nothing terrible happened.

In fact, nothing at all happened. Nobody in Buskin seemed in need of hired help. Several shopkeepers took the opportunity of his inquiry to express the opinion that business in Buskin was lousy and there was little likelihood of his finding employment at all. They were right. He reached the far end of town with his pockets still empty, his belly still empty, and not a single prospect.

Contemplating, he came to the conclusion that his only real hope was to make amends for the mishap at the restaurant. Then maybe Mister Ransom would rehire him.

He went back into the blacksmith shop. The smith, a large black man named Smith, was busy paring the off forehoof of a round-rumped appaloosa. Without looking up, he told Henry, "I just said I can't use you. I got my own sons to help me around here."

"That's not what I wanted to ask, sir," Henry said. "I wanted to ask you, where can I find a lady, name of Miz Maggie?"

Smith dropped the hoof and straightened up. He looked at Henry. His brows climbed his forehead. He pursed his lips, then pointed away from town.

"Out that way a ways. Just follow the beaten path. You'll see a house with a big red ship's lantern on a post in the yard. Nighttime you can see that lamp for miles. That's Miz Maggie's."

"Thank you, sir," Henry said.

As he walked away, he heard Smith begin to laugh. He could still hear the laughter halfway to the house.

Miz Maggie's was a pleasant homey two story frame house painted white with green shutters. A neat white picket fence surrounded it. Morning glories twined around the post that held the lantern.

There was a stable behind the house. As Henry approached, an incredibly ancient stablehand led a saddled horse out and around to the hitchrail in front of the house. The horse was long-legged and coal black. It rolled a wary eye at Henry as he walked past it to the gate.

Inside the picket fence, a flagstone path led through flower beds to a porch surrounded by shrubbery. Henry stepped carefully in the middle of each flagstone for luck. But he didn't feel very lucky. He felt hungry, weary, and a little shaky. When he rapped at the door, his knock sounded weak and uncertain.

The door was opened by an elderly woman in an apron. She had a feather duster in her hand and a rather unpleasant expression on her face. She gave Henry a greeting of "Well?"

"I'd like to see Miz Maggie," he told her.

She looked him down. With a sniff, she said, "Nobody's up yet. Suppose you come back later. In about five years."

With that, she slammed the door.

Sighing, he turned and started down the steps. He almost tripped. His head felt heavy and a little off balance. With another sigh, he seated himself on the bottom step and leaned against the railing. His eyes closed. After a moment, he began to snore.

He was wakened abruptly by something ramming into him, and a startled curse. As he rolled off the step, he glimpsed the man who'd stumbled over him. The man was sitting down very suddenly on the steps.

Henry scrambled to his hands and knees.

The man on the steps got to his feet. He was long and lean and awesome. His hair was black, his brows were black and his moustache was black. His teeth were white and long and sharp. His lips twisted back from them, baring them in a snarl. From where Henry knelt, he looked like a thunderhead ready to spit lightning.

He dusted at his black frock coat and very deliberately shoved back the skirts. He was wearing twin stag handled Colt's revolvers. The guns were fairly new, but the butts already showed wear from handling. He rested his hands on them. Through clenched teeth, he began to curse.

The words pelted down on Henry so hard that he winced at each of them. Clearing his throat, he tried to say he was sorry. The man didn't pay any attention, but just kept cursing.

The door opened. Miz Maggie came out, holding shut her frilly pink wrapper. Her hair was mussed and her eyes were bleary with sleep. She grumbled, "What's going on?"

In a number of choice words, the man told her.

"I'm sorry," Henry said. No one noticed.

The man spoke one more word. It was one Henry had never heard before. He didn't think he ever wanted to hear it again.

"Wade!" Miz Maggie said.

The man snorted through his nose. He looked at Henry. "If I ever lay eyes on you again, you'll be damned sorry of it."

"Yes, sir," Henry agreed.

The man started down the steps.

Henry scrambled out of his way.

He strode on down the walk, slammed open the gate, and flung himself onto the black horse. With a slap of his spurs, he set it into a gallop.

Still on his hands and knees, Henry looked up at Miz Maggie.

"I hope you realize that was Wade Desmond," she told him.

"Ma'am?" he said getting to his feet.

"Wade Desmond. You've heard of him, haven't you?"

"No, ma'am."

"He's the king of the hill. He owns this town, lock, stock and barrel. And he'd as soon step on the likes of you as brush you aside. Now, if you've got any sense at all, you'll get." She aimed a finger into the distance. "Get and don't ever come around here again."

"Please, ma'am, first I got to talk to you . . ."

Henry's voice trailed off. It felt like his stomach was coming apart. He grabbed the stair railing for support. "Unh—can I set down a minute, ma'am? Maybe have a drink of water?"

She eyed him with suspicion based on past experience. He wasn't the first strange youth she'd found in her yard. "You want to get inside and get a free peek, don't you? Listen, you peek and you'll pay just like everybody else."

"Ma'am?"

"Two bits for two peeks. Nothing for free."

"Please, ma'am . . ." Henry mumbled. His head had begun to spin. He felt himself slipping, sliding into a mysterious darkness.

He toppled into the geraniums.

"What on earth?" Miz Maggie said to herself. She called loudly, "Harriet!"

The maid appeared.

"Get some spirits of ammonia and see if you can wake this creature." Miz Maggie indicated Henry.

By the time the maid waved the ammonia under Henry's nose, he was already coming around. Once he was sitting up, Miz Maggie asked him, "What's the matter? You don't have some disease, do you?"

"I reckon I'm mostly hungry," he said. "I ain't had nothing to eat since breakfast yesterday."

"Oh?" Miz Maggie lifted a brow at him. "You're looking for a handout?"

"No, ma'am. I just want to apologize. If you wasn't mad at me, then maybe Mister Ransom would hire me back to work in the restaurant. It was an awful good place to work."

"Oh! You're the young ass who ruined my breakfast yesterday, aren't you?"

"Yes, ma'am. Please, ma'am, let me apologize."

Eyeing him, she said, "You're sure you're not looking for a free peek?"

"A peek at what?" he asked blankly.

"You don't know?"

"No, ma'am."

She studied him. "You really don't know, do you?"

"No, ma'am."

"I'll be damned. Well, come on inside. You can try to explain yourself to me while Sally does my hair."

"Yes, ma'am."

Respectfully, he followed her in.

The house reminded him of Madame Nellie's. It had the same sort of parlor, with deep chaff and love seats. Instead of an organ there was a crank-up nickelodeon, the kind you put a nickel into to get music out of. Over it hung a framed sampler, the crossstitched motto surrounded by carefully embroidered pink rosebuds. It read: *If at first you don't succeed, try, try again.*

A young woman in a flowered wrapper, with rags tied in her hair, was sitting in the parlor running a small file along one fingernail. Miz Maggie called her over.

While the girl was combing curls into Miz Maggie's long blonde hair, Henry told the story of his life. All of it from before his mother died right up to the present moment.

By the time he reached the present, there were four more young women in the room, brushing hair, filing nails, and doing other strange woman-things while they listened. When he finished his story, they asked him questions. They seemed very sweet and sympathetic. All but Miz Maggie.

"You expect me to believe *that?*" she said.

"Yes, ma'am."

"All that hogwash about some professor, and your Uncle Whosis—"

"Uncle Ned."

One of the girls spoke up. "I'll bet I know that professor he's talking about. A red-headed son of a bitch on wheels."

"He's red-headed," Henry told her. "But Uncle Ned said he was a son of a *whore.*"

Miz Maggie chuckled. With a sort of sigh, she handed

108

him a dime. "Go get yourself something to eat at one of the saloons. Then come back here and you can do a few chores to earn that."

"Yes, ma'am!" Henry answered eagerly.

To Miz Maggie's surprise, Henry actually came back. She set him to weeding the geraniums. While he worked, she kept glancing out the window at him.

"A boy his age," she muttered to herself. "And still a virgin?" She said it several times during the course of the morning.

At last, she called him in and asked him outright, "Boy, honestly, are you a virgin?"

"I don't think so," he said. "I think I ain't never been there."

"Where?"

"Virginia."

For a moment, she just looked at him. Then she smiled. It was a very strange smile and it gave Henry a very strange feeling.

"Ah," she said. "It's time someone took you in hand and saw to your proper education."

"Uncle Ned was going to do that, only he went away."

"He could never do it the way I can. But first, you need a bath."

"A bath?"

"Harriet will show you where the bathtub is kept. Bring it up to my room. Have Harriet put on water to boil, and when that's ready, bring it up, too."

"Yes, ma'am."

The tub was a big galvanized thing shaped sort of like a coffin. It had pink posies and gold scrolls painted all over it. Getting it onto his back, Henry lugged it

109

upstairs. Then bucket by bucket, he filled it with water. By the time he was done, he was exhausted.

Miz Maggie tested the water with her fingertips. She took a towel, a bar of Sapolio, and a long-handled brush from her commode.

"Henry," she said. "Get undressed."

"Ma'am?"

"Undressed. You know. Take your clothes off."

"All of them?"

"All of them."

"To the skin?"

"To the skin."

"Ma'am?"

"Yes, Henry?"

"I ain't never undressed in front of nobody. My Maw always said it wasn't right."

"Didn't you ever go swimming with your friends? In a water hole or some such place?"

"Yes, ma'am, only I did it alone. I didn't have no friends. And I kept my drawers on anyway."

Miz Maggie looked a little amused, a little amazed. She asked, "What about when you took a bath? You took your drawers off then, didn't you? You did take baths, didn't you?"

"Yes, ma'am. Only I always done that alone, too."

"Well—uh—what about when you were little? When you were a very little boy, didn't your mother bathe you?"

"Yes, ma'am. As I recall."

"You took your clothes off in front of her, didn't you?"

"Yes, ma'am. I reckon."

"All right. For now, pretend you're a very little boy and I'm your mother. You go ahead and take your clothes off."

110

"Yes, ma'am." Hesitant, but obedient, Henry began to peel. As he stripped off each item, he dropped it neatly into a heap on the floor. He put off his drawers until last. When there was nothing else left to remove, he skinned out of them and stood before Miz Maggie jaybird bare. But try as he might, he just didn't feel the way he had when he was very little and his mother bathed him.

Miz Maggie smiled at him. "Not bad. Turn around."

He turned around.

"Whatever is that?" she said.

"What, ma'am?"

"That hideous mark on your rump."

Henry had never seen the mark, but his mother had mentioned it to him. It was perfectly round, the color of a ripe plum, and almost centered on his left rear cheek.

Embarrassed, he allowed, "It's a birthmark, ma'am. Maw said it was a cannonball on account of the way my Paw died."

"How did your Paw die?"

That was a story Henry's mother had told him often when he was small. Until he'd begun reading Uncle Ned's books, it was the most exciting story he'd ever heard.

"A cannonball went right through his middle," he said. "Purely sliced him right in two."

"In the War of the Rebellion?"

"No, ma'am. On the Fourth of July."

"What?"

"Yes, ma'am. It was the same year I was borned. There was big Fourth of July celebrating and everything in Serenity with a band and a parade and fireworks and all stuff like that. I sure wish I'd been there. I like parades something awful."

111

"What happened to your father?"

"Oh. Yes, ma'am. Paw and another feller took a notion to celebrate by shooting off the courthouse cannon. They loaded it up and wadded it and put in a cannonball. Maw said they'd of left out the cannonball if they'd had any sense. Anyway, they put it in and lit the fuse and the cannon went off, only instead of the ball going out the front the way it was supposed, it come out the back. Blowed the whole back end off the cannon into little pieces." He held up a thumb and forefinger about an inch apart. "And it blowed my Paw right apart with my Maw standing there watching."

"The poor woman!" Miz Maggie exclaimed.

"She was kind of glad of it," Henry said. "Maw always said Paw was a dirty nasty man and it was good riddance and just what he deserved."

"Oh?" Miz Maggie looked taken aback. Then she smiled again. "Well, Cannonball, you climb on into that tub now."

"Into there?" Henry hooked a thumb at the tub.

She nodded.

Reluctantly, he poked a foot into the water. It was hot. But not too hot. He put the other foot in. Slowly, he seated himself.

Miz Maggie handed him the soap and brush. "Now, scrub."

The water turned a scummy gray as he scrubbed. When he got around to his back, Miz Maggie took the soap and brush from him. She had him lean forward while she scoured his spine.

"I recollect my Maw used to wash my back that way when I was little," he told her.

"Do you miss your mother a lot?"

"No, ma'am. I don't reckon so."

"You don't?"

"Once I started getting big, my Maw never paid me much mind. I don't think she liked me very much."

"Come now, Cannonball, I'm sure your mother loved you a lot."

"I reckon so," he allowed. "Only I think she didn't *like* me. Do you know what I mean, ma'am? About her loving me, but not liking me?"

"I certainly do," she answered. "It's a misfortune of a sort that befalls a lot of women. They fall in love with completely insufferable cads and then where are they?"

"Where?"

"Here."

"Here, ma'am?"

Nodding she gave him a rather strange little smile.

"Do you love somebody you don't like, ma'am?" he asked.

"It's been a long long time since I've been in love."

"Was it with one of them kinds of cads you said?"

"Indeed he was. A very insufferable cad, but a completely lovable one. Rather a likable one, as well."

"What become of him?"

She shrugged.

Thinking of the books he'd read, Henry asked, "Do you pine for him, ma'am?"

"Hardly."

According to the books, a woman always pined for a lost love, until she found another. He suggested, "Maybe you ought to get a new beau."

She gave a bit of a snort. "I suppose in a way you might say I have another one."

"Is he one of them kinds of cads, too?"

"A thoroughly insufferable one. Not lovable or even likable by any measure."

113

That bewildered him. It didn't fit with the books at all. "Why do you let him be your beau then?"

"There isn't much alternative, Cannonball. Wade Desmond takes what he wants. If he can't have it, he makes sure no one else can have it either. Last year a stranger came through town with a horse Wade took a fancy to. The man refused to sell, so Wade shot the horse dead. The stranger was just lucky Wade didn't shoot him as well."

"Ain't that against the law?"

"Around here, Wade *is* the law."

"He's a lawman?"

"No. But he's got the lawman cowed. And everyone else. It's Wade and those hounds of his. They ride roughshod over the whole town."

"Hounds?"

"The hard cases that work on that ranch of his. They're always ready to back Wade's hand. If anybody moved against Wade, he'd have them to contend with. So Wade gets whatever he wants. Including me."

She sounded sort of sad. Henry wished he could cheer her up. Still thinking of the books, he said, "Maybe that feller you loved will come to fetch you one of these days."

"Not likely. I doubt if he even remembers me."

"He must, ma'am. You're awful nice. And awful pretty, too. I couldn't never forget you. I wish my Maw had of been like you."

"You do?" She looked oddly at him, and wondered what it would have been like if she'd had a child. Suppose that first time, with her first beau, she'd had a son. He'd have been about this boy's age now. Probably even looked a bit like this boy.

She smiled tenderly at Henry.

114

Nobody had ever looked at him quite like that before. It gave him a funny warm feeling all over. He blurted out, "Ma'am, I sure wish I had of sprung up in your cabbage patch."

"*What!*"

"I wish I had of sprung up in your cabbage patch, Miz Maggie, and been your boy, instead of what I did."

"Cabbage patch! You baby! You poor dumb little piggly!"

With a sudden jerky motion, she got to her feet and turned away from him. Almost harshly, she said, "Get yourself dressed. Then empty that tub and put it back where it came from."

"Yes, ma'am," he mumbled, taken aback at her tone. As he stood up, he asked, "Are you mad at me, Miz Maggie?"

"At you?" she said. "Oh hell no! Not at you, Cannonball."

With that, she left the room.

CHAPTER 15

WHEN HENRY CAME BACK INTO THE PARLOR, MIZ Maggie took one look at his clean-scrubbed face shining above his filthy collar and told him he needed a change of clothes.

Embarrassed, he began to tell her again about his satchel disappearing, and his money as well, and how he didn't have a job, or anything.

She interrupted him. "Do you want a job?"

"Yes, ma'am! Oh, yes, ma'am, I sure do."

"I suppose there's enough work around here to keep a boy busy." As she spoke, she turned her back to him

115

and lifted her skirts. Like Madame Nellie, she had a small gun holster on her garter and a stash of cash hidden in it.

When she faced him again, she held out two dollars. "This is an advance against your wage. Go buy yourself some clothes."

"Yes, ma'am. Uh—er—ma'am?"

"Yes?"

"Can I buy some food, too?"

"It's your money, Cannonball." She smiled at him. "You get yourself whatever you want."

"Yes, ma'am!"

Her face faded. She added, "Just mind you don't run into Wade Desmond."

To Henry's dismay, Wade Desmond proved to be much in evidence in town, appearing from one saloon, strolling along the walk, and disappearing into another briefly, then reappearing. A pair of large rough-looking men decked with revolvers followed close behind him.

Ducking into doorways, hiding behind parked wagons, and detouring entirely around buildings, Henry managed to avoid him completely.

At the General Mercantile, Henry outfitted himself with a full set of work clothes, including fresh drawers. With the bundle under his arm, he watched through the window until he saw Desmond leave the Flying Eagle Saloon and disappear into the Grand Wyoming Palace. As the batwings swung shut behind Desmond, Henry darted for the Flying Eagle. Safe inside, he ordered a couple of sandwiches and even a watered whiskey.

As he sipped his whiskey, he wondered again what had became of Uncle Ned. It sure hadn't been right of Uncle Ned to go and not even say goodbye or leave a message or anything.

Despite the full belly, the warmth of the whiskey, and the pleasure of the bundle under his arm, he felt rather sad as he walked back to Miz Maggie's. But when he got there, she had a surprise for him that cheered him up considerably.

A room of his own.

It wasn't really much of a room, just an enclosed cubby under the staircase intended for storage. But it was his own place in the house. And the cot stuffed into it was more comfortable than his cornshuck mattress back in Missouri had ever been.

Right after supper, Miz Maggie sent him to bed with instructions to stay put there. He didn't object. He dozed almost immediately and was well into a long string of strange dreams when the clatter of feet on the stairs over his head awakened him.

There were other sounds too. The nickelodeon in the parlor was tinkling away, and people were chatting and laughing. It sounded sort of like a playparty. His mother had told him playparties weren't evil in themselves. Especially not the ones held on the church grounds. But she had warned him they could lead to sin.

He wondered if she might have been wrong about that, the same as she had been about so many things. Listening to the laughter, he wished he'd been invited.

When he fell asleep again, he dreamed of the party. For a while, the dream was fun. But then Wade Desmond came into it and did something mean to Miz Maggie and the whole dream got so unpleasant that he woke up from it.

The sounds of the party were gone. He supposed it was over. He lay in darkness, thinking of Miz Maggie, and of Uncle Ned, and of the Professor, and wishing they could all be together.

At last, he slept again.

The next day, Miz Maggie put him back to work in the garden. He spent the morning and a piece of the afternoon weeding and hoeing.

About midafternoon, Miz Maggie called him in. She had him lug the tub up to her room and fill it. Then she told him to strip.

"To wash?" he asked.

"Of course."

"But I only just washed yesterday."

"You'll wash again today, too."

He couldn't see any point in it, but dutifully he bared himself and climbed into the tub. Miz Maggie wielded the brush, scrubbing his back and talking to him. She asked him all kinds of odd questions about his boyhood. It was very strange. She seemed to enjoy giving him the bath, but she got kind of sad about it, too.

The next day was much the same, with chores in the morning and Miz Maggie hustling him into the tub in the afternoon, then sending him to bed early in the evening, before the festivities in the parlor began.

It kept on the same way, day after day, with a bath every day. Henry began to fear for his skin. All that soaping and scrubbing seemed likely to wear it away. But Miz Maggie insisted. Henry supposed it was part of his job and as long as he was taking a wage from her, he had to put up with it.

Before long, he decided it wasn't doing him any serious permanent damage, and it really was kind of fun. Most of his work for Miz Maggie was kind of fun. Only the evenings troubled him.

At first he felt bad about being sent to bed instead of invited to the parties, or at least allowed to watch. But after a time, he began to feel there was something wrong about those parties. Something not at all fun. Something sort of ominous. His dreams about them certainly weren't pleasant.

It was the eve of Independence Day that the sound of angry voices in the hallway wakened him.

"What is it between you and this dumb brat you're keeping here now?" a man demanded. Henry thought the voice was Wade Desmond's.

"Cannonball?" Miz Maggie answered. "He's just a kid I hired to help out around the place."

"Yeah. Sure."

"Of course. What do you think he is?"

"You ain't exactly a spring chicken, Maggie. I know how it is with you old biddies when you get past your prime. You start thinking you can get young again off some truckling kid."

"Wade!"

"Don't think I ain't heard about how he's always sneaking up to your room."

"Sneaking? There's nothing sneaking about it. He cleans up there."

"Cleans up, eh? Is that what you call it?"

"That's what it is. That's *all* it is."

"That better be all."

Footsteps clattered up the stairs over Henry's head. A door slammed. And the night fell silent.

When he finally slept, Henry's dreams were really mean. He woke with the feeling that his presence under Miz Maggie's roof could cause her bad trouble with Wade Desmond.

He was up early, grubbing around in the garden, when the stablehand brought Desmond's saddled horse to the hitchrail. Hiding in the shrubbery, he watched Desmond leave. He wondered if maybe he oughtn't go away somewhere far from Miz Maggie where Wade Desmond could never see or hear of him again. He wondered how far he could get on the six bits he'd saved from his wages.

Miz Maggie called, "Cannonball!"

Shinnying out of the bushes, he faced her. "Yes, ma'am?"

She stood on the porch in her wrapper. Her face looked puffy and tired. She said, "You told me you like parades."

"Yes, ma'am."

"There's going to be one in town today."

"Ma'am!" Thoughts of leaving suddenly faded out of his head.

"Not a very big one, I'm afraid," she warned him. "Buskin isn't a very big town. But we do have a brass band. Half the people in the county who have saddle horses or rigs get duded up to ride in the parade and the other half come to watch. Afterward, there's a picnic and fireworks and a barn dance in the evening."

"Fireworks!"

She smiled. "We'll get you bathed now and you can go on into town. Buy yourself some Chinese crackers if you want. The Mercantile will be open until the parade makes up."

"Ain't you coming, ma'am?"

"The girls and I will drive in later. But there's no need for you to hang around here. It'll be better if you go in alone instead of with us. But mind that you don't run into Wade Desmond. By the time the parade starts, he'll be full of whiskey and itching for some kind of mean nasty fun."

"Yes, ma'am."

"Now fetch the tub up to my room and fill it."

120

"Yes, ma'am!"

Henry had the tub filled and was already halfway undressed when Miz Maggie came into the room. She was still in her wrapper and she seemed uncommon sad for such a festive day. A little distracted, as if she had something unpleasant on her mind. But he was too caught up in the exciting anticipation of the celebration to give it much thought. Peeling his drawers, he started to hop into the tub.

The bedroom door slammed open.

"*So!*"

Wade Desmond stood filling the doorway. His hands were on the butts of his guns. The smell of strong spirits was on his breath.

"Oh God!" Miz Maggie said deep in her throat. Her face looked very pale. "Wade! I can explain!"

"Ain't nothing to explain," he answered thickly. "I can see it all myself. Maggie, Honey, ain't no wetass truckling pup has no part of nothing that belongs to Wade Desmond. Honey, I'm gonna squinch this pup to pieces and wring your scrawny old neck. You hear me?"

"Wade!" she repeated.

He stalked toward her.

Instinctively, Henry tried to step between them.

Desmond swung an open hand at him. It slapped so hard against his head that it sent him sprawling.

Miz Maggie backed away. But Desmond grabbed her shoulder. His fingers clamped hard. He slapped her face.

"Learn you first," he growled. "Then wring your neck."

Henry crouched by the foot of the bed. His head was awhirl. His thoughts were ajumble. He heard Miz Maggie's taut squeal of pain as Desmond slapped her again.

He lunged for Desmond's legs.

Desmond staggered under the impact but caught his balance. Henry tried to grapple him by the knees. Desmond got a leg free and kicked Henry in the chest.

"Squinch you and stomp you to a pulp," he grunted.

Miz Maggie plunged past the two of them and dashed around the end of the bed. On them rested a pair of bright red garters. She snatched the little two-shot pistol from its holster on one garter.

"Wade!" she snapped.

He stopped kicking Henry and turned toward her.

She pointed the tiny gun at him. "Wade, get out of here or I'll shoot."

He laughed. "Shoot, Honey. That thing can't hurt me."

"It can kill you."

"Like hell. *I'll* kill *you*. You and your truckling pup and all your stinking whores. Wring all your damned necks." Hands outheld to grab, he started toward her.

Steadying the pistol in both hands, she pulled the trigger.

In the small room, the shot was like a crack of thunder. It filled the room with smoke. Through watery eyes, Henry saw Desmond flinch and press his hands to his belly.

Through his teeth, Desmond snarled, "You whore! My men'll get you for this!"

Miz Maggie fired again.

A tiny hole appeared in Desmond's forehead. His mouth opened. But he didn't say anything else. He tilted forward and fell to the floor.

"Oh God," Miz Maggie mumbled. She looked at Henry. The little gun was still in her hand, dribbling smoke.

Outside, footsteps sounded on the stairs.

"Cannonball—quick—catch!" She tossed the pistol at him. He caught it.

And suddenly all the girls were crowding into the doorway, staring at Miz Maggie, at Henry, and at the dead body of Wade Desmond.

Miz Maggie took a deep breath, swallowed, and said hoarsely, "Cannonball, you'd better put on your drawers."

CHAPTER 16

IT LOOKED LIKE EVERYBODY IN BUSKIN HAD CROWDED into Miz Maggie's house or was tromping around in her geranium bed. With difficulty, the town marshal kept the sightseers from filling the bedroom and stripping the corpse for souvenirs.

After studying the body, listening to Miz Maggie's description of the incident, and getting confirmation from the girls, the marshal turned to Henry.

"Son," he said. "I'm afraid I'm going to have to arrest you."

"Sir?" Henry was completely confused. The way Miz Maggie told it, it sounded like he, Henry, was the one who'd shot Wade Desmond. He started to say so. But Miz Maggie interrupted him.

"Cannonball," she said, drawing him aside. She leaned close, speaking confidentially. "You do just what the marshal says. Don't ask questions and *don't* say anything."

"Ma'am?"

"There may be trouble from Wade's men. I can't do anything if I'm in jail. It won't matter if you're held a while. Believe me, you'll never be convicted. It probably won't come to a trial. But if it does, if anything goes wrong, I'll speak up. Until then, Cannonball, trust me."

"Yes, ma'am."

She stepped back and spoke for all to hear. "Now you go on with the marshal. It's for your own good. When those hired hands of Wade's hear what's happened, it's best you be in protective custody."

The marshal gave a little grunt, as if he'd had a sudden pain.

Henry said, "Yes, ma'am."

Miz Maggie smiled at him. "You run along with the marshal now."

Still puzzled, but obedient, Henry followed the lawman downstairs and out of the house.

As they threaded through the crowd in the yard, the marshal told him, "Truth is, I ain't sure I can handle it if those hired hands of Desmond's decide to make you guest of honor at a necktie party. Truth is, I could even get bad hurt just trying."

"Yes, sir," Henry agreed, uncomprehending.

The marshal waved toward the tall black horse tied at the hitchrail. "See that animal there? That's the fastest horse in the county. If a man was to jump on him and lay heels to him and take off quick, likely nobody in the county would catch up to him."

"Yes, sir."

The marshal paused. He stood waiting a moment. Henry waited with him. The horse rolled a wary eye at them. After a moment, the marshal walked to the hitchrail and collected the black's reins.

He told Henry, "A man could grab these reins out my hand and pile onto this horse and light out. By time I got my gun unlimbered, he'd be well out of revolver range."

"Yes, sir," Henry said, thinking the marshal must have an awful slow hand or an awful tight holster.

The marshal sighed. He collected his own mount and handed the reins of the black to Henry. "Get on board, boy. We'll ride back to town."

Henry got on board.

The marshal hesitated.

Henry waited.

"Don't you go run off now, boy," the marshal said. He walked around to the far side of his own horse and lifted its forehoof.

The black danced nervously, anxious to be on the move. But Henry held a tight rein on it.

For a long while the marshal stayed bent over fiddling with his mount's hoof. Finally he dropped it and climbed into the saddle. He headed toward town. Dutifully, Henry followed along.

The crowd that had gathered at Miz Maggie's trailed behind at a discreet distance. Close enough to see whatever happened, far enough to be out of range if something did.

The marshal took the long way around, riding behind the stores instead of up the street. At the back door of the jailhouse, he stopped. Henry stopped by his side. He looked at Henry. Then he looked at the mass of spectators tailing along.

Flapping his hands as if he were shooing chickens, he hollered at the crowd, "You get! All of you, go on, get! You're making this poor boy nervous. Get!"

Reluctantly, the crowd broke up. When the last spectator was out of sight, the marshal turned to Henry again. "Now, this here door's bolted from the inside. I'll have to go on around front to get in and open it. I'll leave you wait here without nobody watching you."

"Yes, sir," Henry said.

"You understand me, boy?" the marshal continued. "That horse you're astraddle is good and fast and can go all night. He could have you halfway to the next county afore I ever got that door open. You understand?"

"Yes, sir," Henry said, thinking as how the marshal sure did admire the black horse.

With a discouraged sigh, the marshal lifted rein and rode on down to the end of the row of buildings. He disappeared around the last one.

Henry waited.

Spectators peeked out from behind corners and whispered to each other. Old men muttered. Young men nudged each other with elbows. A small grubby boy hiding behind a rain barrel groped into his pockets. He had a string of penny Chinese poppers he'd been saving for the parade. But this was better than any parade. He located the crackers and a sulphur match. Several people glanced toward him as he struck the match. It fizzled out before the fuse lit. A man in a bowler offered him another. This time the fuse fired. He tossed the string of crackers at the black's heels.

As it hit ground, the poppers began to pop.

The black's rear end went up. Henry grabbed the saddle horn. The black's rear came down and its front went up. Henry hung on for dear life. When its fore-hooves hit ground again, the horse plunged into a headlong gallop.

Startled by what sounded like a spattering of gunshots, the marshal hesitated inside the jailhouse. When the last popper had popped and all was silent, he nudged open the door. He was frowning as he peeked out. Then he saw the black, with Henry still hanging onto the saddle, disappearing into the distance.

With a relieved sigh, he smiled.

By the time the black tired of running, Henry was so far out of sight of Buskin that he had no idea which way the town lay, or how he'd ever get back.

He tried. He felt duty bounden to return to the marshal's custody, to go to jail and perhaps stand trial the way Miz Maggie wanted. He rode and rode and rode, hoping he'd run onto the town, or the railroad tracks, or some wheel ruts, or anything that would guide him back. But come nightfall, he hadn't turned up a trace of the town.

Weary and hungry, he hobbled the black with his belt, rolled himself in the saddle blanket, and slept. When he woke, the horse was gone.

Lugging the saddle, he began to walk.

There was an astonishing sameness to the countryside. The more he walked, the more it all seemed the same. He was in the midst of a vast sea of grass. Everywhichway there was grass. Nothing else. Not a road, not a house. Nothing but grass.

Come nightfall, he rolled himself in the saddle blanket.

The next day, or maybe it was the day after that, he abandoned the saddle. The following day, or maybe the day after that, he somehow lost track of the blanket.

And then he lost track of everything.

Rather suddenly, he opened his eyes and discovered he was under a roof. He was lying on a bed inside a sod shanty and the round rosy-cheeked face of a woman was hovering solicitiously above him.

At the sight of his eyeballs, she smiled and said

127

cheerily, "*Wie sind sie?*"

"Unh?" he groaned.

It was enough of a sign of life to satisfy her. The smile broadened as she told him, "*Ich bin Frau Anna Kaspar.*"

"Ma'am?"

She made a motion over her shoulder. Henry saw then that there was a man standing behind her. The man's face was almost as round as hers, and was trimmed with heavy brows and a full set of whiskers.

"*Herr* Hans Kaspar," the woman told Henry.

"I'm awful hungry," he mumbled in reply.

She frowned slightly and asked the man, "*Ist das ein Name?*"

He shrugged uncertainly, then told Henry, "No speaken the English."

Frau Kaspar bobbed her head in agreement.

Henry tried again with appropriate gestures. "Ma'am. Sir. I'm awful hungry."

"*Ach!*" Frau Kaspar said. She nodded comprehension and scurried off. In a moment she was back with a tin mug full of milk.

At the sight of it, Henry dragged himself into a sitting position. He grabbed for the mug with both hands, emptied it and gestured for more.

Frau Kaspar dashed off to fetch the pitcher.

Herr Kaspar nodded to himself. He was satisfied that the stray he'd found was well enough and strong enough to be put to earning his keep in a day or two.

Henry tried to explain that he really ought to go back to Buskin and wait in jail, perhaps stand trial, the way Miz Maggie wanted. The Kaspars didn't understand a word he said.

Herr Kaspar tried to explain that he was offering the husky healthy youth a permanent position as a hired hand. Henry didn't understand a word he said.

But Herr Kaspar's gestures conveyed the impression that he wanted Henry to work.

And Henry felt an obligation to do so. After all, he'd eaten the Kaspars' food and slept under their roof. They might even have saved his life. He had a debt to them.

And he didn't know the way back to Buskin.

The farm wasn't much like his mother's, but the chores were similar. He got the hang of it all easily enough. Herr Kaspar seemed pleased with his work. And Frau Kaspar was a good cook. With three meals a day and a cozy pallet in the cowshed, he decided it likely wouldn't do any harm if he stayed on until the fall harvest was in. He told himself he'd leave then, before the first snow, and find his way back to Buskin somehow.

Only the next day his plans got changed.

The roof of the Kaspars' house was made of poles and planks chinked with mud and covered over with cut sods. With gestures, Herr Kaspar indicated for Henry to go up and plug the holes where daylight showed through.

Carrying a bucket of mud, Henry clambered up the ladder and set to work. One moment he was standing in the sunshine, happily slapping mud into the leaky places. The next moment, he was falling, crashing into the Kaspars' brass-frame bed, and then the bed was collapsing on top of him.

Overhead, the sun shone brightly through a large hole in the roof.

With a squeal of concern, Frau Kaspar began to dig Henry out of the debris of the bed. Herr Kaspar hurried to help her. Together they got Henry onto his feet. But when they let go, he discovered he couldn't stand up. Something very painful was wrong with his right leg.

Frau Kaspar killed a chicken and set about making soup while Herr Kaspar splinted Henry's broken shin. During the next few weeks, the Frau paused regularly in her chores to fetch Henry a steaming bowl of soup, and the Herr paused regularly in his chores to curse the fickleness of fate.

By the time Henry was on his feet again, the first snow had fallen and was forgotten under a thick blanket of white. Not only was Henry snowed in, he was thoroughly indebted to the Kaspars. There was no possible returning to Buskin before spring.

The Kaspars' house was warm and their larder was full. Henry learned the Frau's names for many of the foods she set before him, and the Herr's names for most of the farm animals. He wondered if, given time, he might not be able to learn enough of their words to actually talk to them. He thought it would be very pleasant to stay on with them as long as they'd have him.

But as the sun grew warmer and the snow turned to mud, he kept recollecting Miz Maggie and the debt he owed her.

He couldn't bring himself to desert the Kaspars before the spring plowing was done. But once the last furrow had been cut, he set about trying to explain that he was duty bounden to return to Buskin.

Once he got it across to the Kaspars that he meant to leave, the Frau threw her arms around him, squeezing so hard that his face turned red. Then she made up a bundle of bread and sausage for him to take along.

Herr Kaspar gave him a dollar in coin and a

thoughtful lecture on the problems and duties of a young man leaving home to see the world. Henry didn't understand a word of it.

With his dollar, his lunch, and an old quilt the Frau insisted he take, Henry set out in the direction Herr Kaspar indicated. He walked steadily, pausing only to eat. By nightfall, he hadn't come to anything. He hadn't even seen a sign of anything. Curled in his quilt, he slept on the ground.

The next day he spotted an object on the horizon. As he got closer, he recognized it for a railroad water tank.

The third day, he arrived at a town of sorts. Under the water tower there was a general store, a church, and a combination railroad and telegraph station. And there were people who spoke English.

When the boomer presently in charge of the key and the tank found out Henry had a dollar in cash, he offered to arrange Henry's passage to Buskin for exactly that amount.

Henry paid up.

That night, when the late freight stopped for water, the boomer slipped a brakeman fifty cents to stow Henry in an empty cattle car.

It was almost dawn and Henry was asleep when the train pulled into Buskin. He was jounced awake as the locomotive maneuvered its burden into the wye to let the westbound express go past. As the car stopped moving, the door slid open.

The brakeman called in a harsh half-whisper, "All right, kid, this is it."

"It?"

"Your stop. Buskin, Wyoming. Hop out quick and don't let anybody see you."

"Yes, sir." Henry hopped out quick. Heeding the brakie's advice, he slunk cautiously away from the tracks. He wasn't sure why he had to be so careful not to be seen, but he supposed there was a good reason. He kept slinking all the way to Miz Maggie's house.

It was still too early for anyone to be up and around inside the house, so he crept under the bushes to wait, and fell asleep.

The clatter of spurred boots on the porch woke him. Rising on his knees, he peered from his hiding place. Two horses stood ready at the hitchrail. Two men strode down the flagstone path toward them. Henry recognized the men. He'd seen them around the saloons last year when he'd lived in Buskin himself.

"Hey, you there!"

Flinching, Henry looked toward the voice. The maid, Harriet, was on the porch. She'd spotted him. She snapped, "You, in the bushes, get out of there!"

Henry got to his feet.

Harriet scowled at him. She said, "Cannonball?"

The two men had turned to see what was happening. One of them gave a shout. "It's the Cannonball Kid!"

"He's back!" the other hollered.

"Come on, we got to tell the town!"

Both men jumped onto their horses and headed off at a gallop.

"Boy," Harriet said. "Is Miz Maggie gonna be surprised to see you."

CHAPTER 17

HARRIET SNIFFED AT THE AROMA OF CATTLE CAR AND said, "You wait out here. I'll fetch Miz Maggie."

Henry waited.

Miz Maggie came rushing out clutching her wrapper

around her. She looked at Henry with an expression he couldn't comprehend.

"It *is* you," she said.

"Yes, ma'am."

"What the devil did you have to come back for?"

"I thought you—"

"Did anybody see you come into town?"

"Just the man on the train, ma'am."

"Good."

"But a couple of fellers seen me here in your yard. They rode off somewheres hollering."

"Oh oh. Cannonball, you'd better come on inside." She led him into the hallway. Wrinkling her nose, she told him, "You'd better get out the tub and take it up to my room."

"Am I gonna take a bath?"

"Yes indeed."

Obediently, Henry hustled the tub upstairs. He was about to go back down for water when he heard the commotion. Stepping to the bedroom window, he looked down into the yard.

People were gathering just like when Wade Desmond was killed. Galloping up on horseback, rattling up in wagons, and racing up afoot, they crowded into the yard and stomped around in the geraniums.

Miz Maggie stepped out of the house to face them. Henry couldn't see her for the roof of the porch, but he heard her call loudly for quiet.

Nobody responded.

"Shut up!" she roared.

They yammered on.

Drawing the pistol from its holster on her garter, she fired into the air.

She got their attention. The chattering faded to a

133

murmur. The crowd looked porchward.

Miz Maggie announced, "Yes, The Kid is here. But he's tired. He's had a long hard trip and he wants to rest and refresh himself. Please, all of you go away. Let him have some peace and quiet."

"We want to see him!" a man called from the mob.

Others echoed the sentiment.

"Not now," Miz Maggie answered.

"If we go away now, can we come back and see him later?"

She hesitated.

Others in the crowd took up the question, shouting it at her.

At last, she allowed, "I suppose so."

"When?"

"Later."

"When later?"

"Tomorrow," she suggested.

Moans and groans and flat refusals answered her.

She insisted, "Give The Kid a chance, will you? Let him rest a while."

Someone in the mob replied, "We'll give him till noon. Then we're gonna see him in person!"

Others backed this declaration.

"Noon then," Miz Maggie sighed.

Reluctantly, the crowd broke up.

What was all that about? Henry wondered as he went on downstairs to fetch his bath water. He had the tub filled and was stripping his clothes when Miz Maggie came into the bedroom.

"Now, why the devil did you come back here?" she said. "Because of the books?"

"Books?" he said blankly.

"You have heard of The Cannonball Kid, haven't you?"

"No, ma'am."

"No? Then why did you come back?"

"I thought you wanted me to. I thought you wanted me to go to jail and maybe stand trial and all, like you said after Mister Desmond got killed."

She shook her head slowly.

Befuddled, he asked, "You *don't* want me to go to jail?"

"There's no need of it now," she said. "Wade's hired men are gone, and the coroner's jury decided his death was unintentional suicide."

"What's that?"

"They said in going up against The Cannonball Kid, he committed suicide, but since he didn't know you were The Kid, it was unintentional. They could hardly press charges against someone like The Kid. The case is closed."

He found himself even more befuddled. "The Cannonball Kid, ma'am?"

"I'll explain it all to you, but you've got to promise me you'll keep it a secret."

"Yes, ma'am."

"No one must ever know the truth. *No one.*"

"Not even Uncle Ned and The Professor?"

"You found that wayfaring uncle of yours?"

"No, ma'am. But I will. Someday. I think."

She smiled sympathetically, thinking it exceedingly unlikely he'd ever locate the uncle who'd abandoned him. "All right, you can tell him when you find him, but no one else. Understand?"

"Yes, ma'am."

"Swear it to me."

He raised one hand and put the other over his heart. "I swear it, ma'am. I won't tell nobody else in the whole world."

He settled into the tub. As Miz Maggie scrubbed his back, she told him how she'd been sure Desmond's hired hands would raise hell about his killing. Frightened for herself as well as for Henry, she'd decided to try spooking them. She'd started a rumor.

She spread the story that Henry wasn't actually what he seemed. She told one and all that he was really The Cannonball Kid.

According to her story, The Kid was a protector of the weak and innocent, a figure so fabulous that villains fled at the threat of him. To get his quarry to stand and face him, he often had to masquerade as a callow youth.

The way she told it, The Kid had come to Buskin specifically to rid the town of Desmond's domination. Once Desmond was dead, The Kid would go after his hired hands.

The story caught on instantly. Even the girls in the house believed it. Sally had been so taken by it that she'd put the story of Desmond's death into ballad form on the spot. By nightfall, the song had spread to every saloon in town. The more imaginative townsfolk were recounting other tales of The Kid's adventures and swearing to the veracity of them.

By the time Desmond's crew got word of their boss's death, they got a lot more as well. Nobody around Buskin had seen horn nor hoof of any of them since.

"The story served its purpose. I thought that was the end of the matter," Miz Maggie said with a sigh. "But after a few months, the books began showing up."

"Books?" Henry asked.

She went to the dresser, took a little yellow-covered paperback book from a drawer, and held it out for him to see.

The etching on the cover showed a young man in a

shield-front shirt and hairy Montana-style chaps, with a huge peaked sombrero on. He was holding a smoking six-shooter out in front of him. Across from him, three very evil looking men with heavy black beards and lots of knives and revolvers were collapsing into a cloud of dust. In the background a pretty young woman clutched her hands prayerfully to her bosom.

The title read *The Cannonball Kid: A True Story Of Astonishing Heroism On The Wild Western Frontier.* The author's name was given as Colonel Buck McGunn. The price was ten cents.

"That's about *me?*" Henry asked.

"No. But it's about the person everybody around here *thinks* you are."

It was all very confusing. Studying the cover, he said, "Who's this Mister Colonel Buck McGunn?"

"I have absolutely no idea." She returned the book to the dresser. "Probably some bald old coot behind a desk in Boston or New York who's never been West of Cincinnati. From the details in his books, I'd guess he heard Sally's song somewhere and it inspired him. Now there seems to be a new book of The Cannonball Kid's adventures every month."

She sighed again. "The whole thing has gotten out of hand. The Cannonball Kid is the hero of all Buskin. For all I know, he's the hero of the whole United States by now. And you've gone and made it worse by coming back here."

"Ma'am?"

"You could go anywhere else in the entire world and no one would ever suspect *you* of being the hero of those books. But here in Buskin, you're known. People all think you really are the person this McGunn is writing about." She paused, then added, "Cannonball, if you turn out to be just plain Henry Caleb Lacey, Junior, it's going to be a terrible disappointment to folks."

"What should I do, ma'am?"

"For now, perhaps you could bluff it out. We'll show you off to folks at noon, then get you out of town as fast as we can. Eventually it'll all blow over. As long as you stay away from Buskin, everything should be fine."

"Yes, ma'am. I'll try."

"Good boy. Just remember, let me do all the talking."

"Yes, ma'am."

When she was done scrubbing his back, Henry climbed out of the tub and reached for his clothes.

"No," she said with a shake of her head. "You can't wear those rags."

"They're all I got. When I come to Buskin the first time, I had a satchel, only I took it into—"

"Don't tell me about your satchel again. Just a minute." She pulled the covering from a large object in the corner. The object proved to be a massive wardrobe trunk. As she opened it, she said, "A barnstorming actor left this some time ago in payment of his bill. It's full of costumes. Maybe there's something suitable."

He watched her haul odd clothing out of the trunk. A bright red tunic with brass buttons and gold colored epaulets caught his eye, but Miz Maggie insisted his outfit should be tastefully simple. She chose the plain gray suit the actor had worn as Asa Trenchard in *Our American Cousin.*

Henry tried the suit on. The actor evidently had been about his weight but somewhat shorter. Henry's wrists protruded from the sleeves and the trousers revealed his ankles. Even so, he felt rather proud of his reflection in the mirror.

Long before noon, the crowd began to gather in Miz Maggie's yard. By the time the stationmaster's big brass turnip indicated exactly twelve o'clock, Union Pacific time, everybody from twenty or thirty miles of Buskin was standing in front of the house waiting.

Miz Maggie went out onto the porch first. She made a little speech. Then she opened the door and beckoned for Henry. With a heavy lump in his gullet, he stepped to her side.

The crowd raised a rousing cheer. A few men shot off guns. Older kids fired blank cartridge pistols and younger ones rattled rocks in tin cans. Babes in arms squawled in alarm. A young woman some months pregnant fainted. A loosely tied saddle horse ran away.

Just as he'd rehearsed, Henry nodded and bowed. He felt shaky scared, but pleasantly excited, too. Not even at his mother's funeral had so many people paid so much attention to him. They applauded and cheered him.

He nodded and bowed some more.

They applauded and cheered some more.

A balding man in a claw hammer coat came clumping up the steps. He was carrying a crudely whittled wooden key about two feet long. Holding it out, he informed Henry, "I am Samuel Howland. It is my privilege to be the Mayor of the Proud and Gracious City of Buskin."

"How do, sir," Henry said, bobbing his head in respect. He'd never met a Mayor before.

The Mayor cleared his throat. Turning to face the crowd, he proclaimed, "On behalf of the Fair City of Buskin, The Flowering Rose of Wyoming, The Eventual Foremost Metropolis of The West, I wish to present you with this Key To The City."

The crowd cheered and applauded.

The Mayor thrust the wooden key into Henry's hands. He said, "We have a small fete in your honor planned for tonight at Meisner's barn. There'll be dancing and dining and a general celebration in appreciation of our honored guest."

"He can't come," Miz Maggie said quickly.

"What!" The Mayor looked terribly taken aback.

"He's got to go," she said. "He's got business elsewhere."

"He's got to come." The Mayor turned to Henry. "What about it, Mister Cannonball Kid? You will come, won't you? It's in your honor. Folks have already started fixing up the vittles."

The word vittles did something to Henry's insides. It had been a long time since he finished the last of Frau Kaspar's sausages. And in all the hubbub of preparing him for his public showing, Miz Maggie had never thought to feed him.

In behalf of his stomach, he allowed, "I reckon I could stay long enough for vittles."

The crowd applauded and cheered.

Miz Maggie scowled and contemplated kicking him in the shin. But it was too late for that now. He was publicly committed.

CHAPTER 18

MIZ MAGGIE HAD LITTLE HOPE OF PREVENTING disaster that night, but at least she could try. She gave Henry half a dozen different dime novels, all of them about the adventures of The Cannonball Kid, and told him to study them as if his life depended on them.

Settled in her bedroom with a book in one hand and a sandwich in the other, he began to read. The book turned out to be so exciting that he kept forgetting the sandwich. It was hard to imagine himself doing such things and saying such things as the hero of the book did and said, but it was fun to try.

When Miz Maggie came to get him ready for the celebration he'd finished the first book and was well into the second. Reluctantly, he dog-eared the page he was on and put the book down. He was sorry now he had promised to go to the party. He'd much rather stay here and read about The Cannonball Kid.

Miz Maggie had a present for him. A brand new white Stetson. She combed his hair for him, parting it down the middle and slicking it in place with sweet scented pomade. She adjusted his linen collar, tied his cravat, then topped him off with the Stetson. Stepping back, she considered him critically.

"You'll do," she told him. "If you'll only keep your mouth shut."

Lips compressed, he nodded in sincere promise.

Meisner's barn was fancied up with lanterns and streamers. A good crowd was already on hand when Henry arrived with Miz Maggie and the girls. Word spread the instant he stepped down from Miz Maggie's carriage. The mob surged out to greet him. It engulfed him. He was swept along by it and—to his horror— separated from Miz Maggie.

Somebody handed him a glass. He gulped from it and discovered it contained whiskey. Taken in moderation, strong spirits were man's friend. He gulped some more. A warm pleasant feeling began to grow in him.

People around him pumped his hand and clapped him

on the back. Some asked questions about his exploits. He forgot his promise to Miz Maggie and answered them with snippets from the book he'd just read.

Somebody gave him another glass of whiskey. He emptied it. He was on his third drink when Miz Maggie managed to reach him. She tried to drag him away from his admirers but he didn't want to go. He was feeling real good now, and he was enjoying all the questions. It wasn't hard to answer them. He just pretended he really was The Cannonball Kid and words came right out.

After a while the Mayor got everybody quieted down enough for the dancing to start. As soon as the squares began to make up, the Mayor rushed over to Henry. He was dragging along a young lady in white ruffles. She looked about Henry's age. Her hair was chestnut with glints of gold in its curls. Her eyes were a sort of green and when she turned them on Henry, he thought they must be exactly what Colonel Buck McGunn meant by limpid.

"My daughter, Lavinia," the Mayor said.

Miss Lavinia held out a hand.

Warm with whiskey, Henry remembered what Uncle Ned had taught him at Madame Nellie's. He took the hand gently and bowed, pressing his lips to her knuckles.

She giggled.

The Mayor beamed.

Miz Maggie looked on in astonishment.

"I'm certain you two young people would like to dance," the Mayor suggested.

Henry couldn't remember a thing about dancing being mentioned in the book he'd read. He stammered, "I—uh—er—"

"I suppose you have small opportunity for such

pastimes, Mister Cannonball Kid," Miss Lavinia said sweetly.

Henry turned red.

"It's very easy," she continued. "You come on. I'll show you how."

Clutching his hand, she hauled him onto the floor. She shoved him into a forming square and took her place beside him.

The fiddle squealed and the caller began to drone, "Honor your corners, honor your partners, all join hands and circle round."

After a while Henry decided his mother had been completely mistaken about the evils of dancing. It was downright fun and not all that hard either. He kind of tripped a couple of times and he never quite caught up with the rest of the square, but he bounced gaily in time to the music and beamed at Miss Lavinia, and she smiled back at him so pretty that he just knew he was doing fine.

Once the set was done, she got a grip on his hand again. Dragging him toward the punch bowl, she told him, "I'm just awfully thirsty."

He saw men ladling up cups of punch for their ladyfriends. Emulating them, he fetched one for her.

Between sips, she told him, "For a beginner, you dance divinely, Mister Cannonball Kid."

"Uh—er—I—"

"I hope you won't think I'm just awfully forward," she said. "But would you mind terribly if I called you Cannonball?"

"Uh—er—I—"

"And you call me Lavinia."

"Uh—er—I—Miss Lavinia," he managed.

She smiled coyly. "It sounds pretty the way you say it."

His head was spinning a bit. Uncle Ned rushed into his thoughts. So did the Professor. One or the other put words on his tongue. "It's real pretty. And so are you, Miss Lavinia."

She giggled.

The fiddle called for another set of squares. Grabbing Henry's hand, she tugged him into one. As she stepped to his side, she told him, "Don't you be shy now. All you need is practice."

"Yes, ma'am, Miss Lavinia," he agreed, warmly certain she was right.

The evening somehow disappeared in a swirl of lights and music and clinking glasses and Miss Lavinia's smile. Henry didn't remember how he got back to Miz Maggie's at all.

He woke suddenly on his old cot under the stairs with his head sort of achy and his mouth tasting like sour ashes, and a feeling like all kinds of real nice recollections were lurking just out of sight in the back of his mind.

He found Miz Maggie in the parlor with the girls. The sun was shining brightly through the windows. It was coming from the wrong direction for morning. Blinking and squinting, he mumbled, "I must of slept late."

"Indeed you did," Miz Maggie said. She looked around at the girls. "The Kid and I would like to be alone."

Tittering among themselves, the girls rose and filed out of the room with many an admiring glance at Henry. Once they were gone, Miz Maggie motioned for him to seat himself.

"Cannonball," she told him. "You're a marvel. It was wonderful."

"Ma'am?"

"Last night. You pulled it off perfectly. It was as though you actually were Cannonball Kid. You were saying all the right things and doing all the right things. How on earth did you do it?"

Henry felt his face flush. He couldn't recall anybody ever saying such nice things about him before. He said, "I don't know, ma'am. I been reading them books. I reckon I just sort of done what he'd of done. I mean the feller in the books."

"You have hidden depths, Cannonball. Or at least hidden talents. You've missed your calling. You should have gone into the theater."

"I did once. I went into the Bella Union in San Francisco with Uncle Ned and Mister Fishfoot."

She cocked a brow at him, then smiled and said, "Well, now, are you ready to travel?"

"Ma'am?"

"There's a good horse saddled and waiting in the stable for you. I want you to get as far from Buskin as you can. New York should be nice this time of year. Or you might go back to San Francisco. You could hunt this Uncle Whosis of yours. I think—"

A rap at the door interrupted her. She listened to Harriet's footsteps, then a murmur of voices. In a moment Harriet came into the parlor and announced, "It's Mister Hooper, ma'am. He says he's got to see The Cannonball Kid. He's got something for him."

Miz Maggie gave a disgusted snort. Turning to Henry, she asked, "Do you think you can handle it?"

"Ma'am?"

"Pretend you're The Cannonball Kid again."

"Oh. Yes, ma'am. It's easy."

"All right. Harriet, show Mister Hooper in."

Hooper was a small elderly man with a large gray

145

moustache and very sad eyes. He ran the General Mercantile. He was carrying a package wrapped in brown paper, tied with twine. He held it out in front of him in both hands as if it were extremely precious.

"Miz Maggie. Mister Cannonball Kid," he said, giving little nods of greeting.

"The Kid's tired, Hooper," Miz Maggie said. "He had a hard night. Can you make it quick?"

"Yes, ma'am. Oh, yes, ma'am!" Hooper began unlacing his parcel. He brought out a black buscadero belt with two holsters crammed full of Colt's Peacemakers.

Holding the belt out with the gunbutts toward Henry, he said respectfully, "These were Wade Desmond's. After he died, there didn't any heirs come to claim 'em so the town held a drawing. I won 'em. Had 'em in my store window for show. But I figure rightfully they ought to belong to you. I'm grateful to you, Mister Cannonball Kid. Desmond used to come into my place, buy everything I had on his chit and never pay up. I'm sure grateful to you."

Blushing, Henry made uncertain noises in his throat.

Mistaking Henry's embarrassment for gentlemanly modesty, Hooper turned to Miz Maggie. "Ain't he grand?"

Miz Maggie coughed as if she were choking on something. Catching her breath, she told Henry, "Go ahead, Cannonball, take them."

Henry accepted the guns.

Hooper reached into his parcel again. This time he brought out a bright blue shield front shirt. Then a pair of striped saddle pants. After that a pair of white woolly Montana style winter chaps. "These are a present from me. I figured you could likely use a new outfit and I had 'em

146

all on my shelves. Got six more pair of them fuzzy chaps. There wasn't nobody around here who'd wear the things. They all laughed their fool heads off at the sight of 'em. I reckon they'll laugh different now when they see you wearing 'em, eh, Mister Cannonball Kid?"

"Gee," Henry said.

"The Kid's much obliged," Miz Maggie told Hooper. "Now, you'd better get. The Kid's got to leave pretty quick."

"Leave town!" Hooper was taken aback.

"Yes."

"He *can't* leave! Not now!"

"He's got to," she said.

"No!" he insisted. "Miz Maggie, he just *can't*. When the train stopped for dinner, the passengers heard about him being here and half of 'em decided to stay over till the next train so's they could get a look at him. They bought up every copy of the Cannonball Kid books I had in stock. He's *got* to come into town and be seen, else there's gonna be a mess of disappointed people. Maybe even a riot. They might want me to take all them books back."

"Hell," Miz Maggie mumbled.

"You're his friend," Hooper continued. "You can talk him into staying. The town would be mighty obliged if you'd do it. I'd take it as a personal favor, ma'am."

Miz Maggie sighed.

Hooper turned to Henry. "Please, sir, you can stay a while, can't you?"

Nobody had ever called Henry sir before. He really wanted to repay Mister Hooper's kindnesses.

Inside his head, he asked himself what the real Cannonball Kid would do in such a situation. Aloud, he answered, "I reckon I owe it to all them folk to oblige them."

147

"Oh no!" Miz Maggie groaned softly.

Hooper grinned and grabbed Henry's hand. As he pumped it he said, "You won't regret this, sir! I promise you. Anything you need besides what I brought you, you just come on into my store and pick it out. I'll let you have it at my cost."

"Thank you, sir," Henry said.

Hooper darted a glance upward. He looked to Miz Maggie. "Ma'am, I know it's kinda early for business, but as long as I got somebody minding the store and I'm here now and all I was kinda thinking maybe—uh— would Miss Marthy be in to company now?"

Automatically, Miz Maggie gave him her warm professional smile and said, "Why, I'm sure the dear girl would be delighted to see you."

Rigged up in his new outfit and fortified with brandy, Henry mounted the horse Miz Maggie had secured for his getaway. Miz Maggie followed behind him in her carriage, keeping a hopeful watchful eye on him.

Word preceded their arrival in town. Crowds lined the street. At the sight of Henry, they began to cheer.

Unnerved, his horse pranced and danced the length of town before Henry could get it in hand and get himself out of the saddle. As his feet touched ground the mob pressed around him. People thrust copies of Colonel Buck McGunn's books at him, asking him to sign them.

Obligingly, he started to scribble *Henry Caleb Lacey, Junior* across the first one. Fortunately he broke the point of the pencil. Somebody offered him another, but he felt bounden to repair the one he'd broken. By the time he'd borrowed a knife and whittled a new point, he realized it wasn't Henry Caleb Lacey, Junior's name folks wanted written on their books, but The Cannonball Kid's.

He wasn't sure he ought to go writing a name that wasn't rightly his own. But Miz Maggie had told him there wasn't any real Cannonball Kid except him. And people were being so nice that he hated to disappoint them. So he carefully scrawled *The Cannonball Kid* across each yellow cover that was held out toward him. By the time he'd done it to them all, his hand was stiff and aching.

Ramming through the crowd, the Mayor arrived in front of Henry. He grabbed Henry's hand and began to pump. Henry winced.

"Oh, sorry!" the Mayor said. "I like to forgot that's your shooting hand. I hope I didn't hurt it."

"It's a mite cramped from all that writing," Henry told him.

"Terrible!" he sympathized. "A calamity. Mister Cannonball Kid, what I came to say is that my daughter, Lavinia—you remember Lavinia?"

"Yes, sir!" Henry said, reddening.

"My daughter, Lavinia, and I would be pleased for your company to supper tonight."

"I don't think I can come."

"Why, of course you can!" the Mayor insisted. "We're expecting you. Lavinia is planning to prepare the meal with her own two sweet hands, just for you. You've got to—"

Suddenly somebody was elbowing the Mayor aside. He was a dark-eyed unshaven young man in range clothes. He had a cud of tobacco between his teeth. Shoving it into his cheek, he looked up and down and said, "So you're this Cannonball Kid I been hearing so much about."

"Yes, sir," Henry smiled.

"Well, I'm Butch Bailey."

A murmuring in the crowd suggested that the name

was familiar to at least a few of the spectators.

"I'm pleased to meet you, Mister Bailey." Henry offered his hand.

Bailey ignored it. He told Henry, "Folks in Arizona know me for a hard man. I've killed six men, three of 'em in fair fights. I say you ain't so much. I say you and me step out into the street and settle right now which of us is the best man."

A hush came over the crowd.

Henry said, "Sir?"

"Sir!" the Mayor exclaimed. "Unthinkable! Impossible!"

Bailey looked askance at the Mayor. "He's scared?"

"I'm afraid The Cannonball Kid's hand is not in any condition for such an encounter at the moment," the Mayor answered.

"He's scared," Bailey said.

"Never!" the Mayor continued in Henry's behalf. "He will be happy to meet you tomorrow, I'm sure. But he's got to have time for his hand to recover from today's ordeal. Besides, he's having supper with my daughter and me tonight."

Bailey worked his cud and spat in the dust at Henry's feet. Curling a lip, he said, "Tomorrow then?"

"Of course," the Mayor said. He looked to Henry.

Dutifully, Henry nodded agreement.

CHAPTER 19

MIZ MAGGIE WAS APPALLED.

Henry didn't exactly understand why, or what it was he had agreed to do, besides have supper with the Mayor and Miss Lavinia. When Miz Maggie explained

150

it all to him, he lost his appetite.

Back in her parlor, sipping a watered brandy while she downed one straight, he asked her, "Ma'am, what should I do?"

"There's one simple solution to the problem," she told him. "Just get on your horse and get."

"I can't do that. I done went and promised."

"Don't you understand? You could get k—uh—hurt."

"Yes, ma'am," he allowed. "Only I've give my word and I can't go back on it."

Miz Maggie made a small sound of exasperation. She said, "Cannonball, of all the people in the world, why did you have to be you?"

"Ma'am?"

She didn't answer. She poured herself another drink, downed a good part of it, and looked thoughtfully out the window. After a while, she muttered, "Maybe there is a chance."

"Ma'am?" he asked.

"Just a minute," she said. She left the parlor and he heard footsteps clatter up the stairs. When she came back she was carrying a belt and holster an urgent customer had once left in pawn against his debt. He had never reclaimed it and never would. The following day he had met his demise in an ill-timed shooting incident.

The outfit didn't look like much to Henry. It wasn't nearly as fancy as the rig that had come with Wade Desmond's guns. Then Miz Maggie showed him what was special about it.

The holster opened up like a clamshell. A set of springs held it shut while it was empty or a gun was at rest in it. But if the wearer grabbed for the gun it held, springs snapped the front open and almost threw the gun into his hand. Quick as the gun cleared leather, the holster snapped shut again.

"You think you can manage it?" Miz Maggie asked him.

He looked doubtful. "I ain't exactly too handy."

"That's what I'm afraid of. But it's worth trying. Come on along, let's see how you do."

In the backyard, with an unloaded gun, Henry gave it a try. Oddly, he got the hang of it right off, not once dropping the gun.

Somewhat encouraged, Miz Maggie had him put a round in the cylinder. She set a bottle on the chopping block behind the stable and told him to try hitting it.

He got the gun out of the holster just fine. He got his finger on the trigger and his thumb on the hammer, and even got the hammer back to full cock. His finger jerked against the trigger.

The bullet flew off somewhere clear past the far end of the stable.

"It's all right," Miz Maggie said soothingly. "You're nervous. Try again. This time take it easy. Don't hurry. Set your sights and squeeze the trigger gently."

"Yes, ma'am," Henry said. He loaded up, settled the gun in the holster and let his hand hang at his side.

Miz Maggie counted to three.

The gun jumped into Henry's hand. Leveling it, he took careful aim. Gently, he fired.

Lead spanged off the stable roof.

Miz Maggie drew a breath between her teeth. She held a hand toward him. "Here, let me show you."

He gave her the gun and holster. She wrapped the belt around her middle, positioned herself, mumbled something about being out of practice, and told him to give her the count.

Marking each number on his fingers, he said, "One, two, three."

Quicker than he could see it, the gun was in Miz Maggie's hand, blasting powdersmoke and noise. And the bottle neck was flying apart.

"Gee," he said. "That's awful good shooting."

"Nothing to it." Miz Maggie gave the gun a twirl and slid it back into the holster. "You ought to see me with a rifle."

"I'd like to, ma'am."

"But not now. Right now, you've got to learn to do it yourself."

As Henry returned the rig to his own middle, he said, "I—uh—I think maybe I ain't got the feel for it. Or the eye for it. Or something."

"Nonsense," she assured him. "All you need is practice."

So he practiced.

He kept on drawing and firing. It all became one graceful motion, the gun appearing in his hand, blasting as it arrived there. Then, on the twenty seventh round, he succeeded in hitting the wall of the stable. He placed the slug within six yards of his target.

Miz Maggie sighed and allowed, "I don't think one day of practice will do it. You'd better let that pistol cool off. Come on into the house and we'll try to think of something else."

They sat in the parlor, sipping brandy and thinking. But neither one had thought of anything by the time Henry had to leave for the Mayor's supper.

With trepidation, Miz Maggie watched him ride off into the lowering shadows.

The Mayor and Miss Lavinia lived in a cottage on the far side of town. With a hearty welcome, the Mayor led

153

Henry into the parlor. Miss Lavinia appeared from the kitchen just long enough to smile and say hello. The Mayor handed Henry a drink, then sat down and began to tell him about The Fair City of Buskin, its Promising Future, and Potential Position in the World. Keeping up his own end of the conversation was no problem to Henry. All he had to do was nod when the Mayor paused.

Then Miss Lavinia rang a tiny bell and they went into the dining room. Miss Lavinia served. The food was good and there was a lot of it. Henry kept stuffing his mouth while the Mayor continued his expostulation on the wonders of Buskin, and Miss Lavinia darted him coy smiles.

When the meal was done, the Mayor and Henry retired to the parlor for more drinks. The Mayor was still talking about Buskin when Miss Lavinia came in and mentioned how pretty the moonlight was.

The next thing Henry knew, he was outside, walking through the night with Miss Lavinia's hand holding his. For a while, they walked in silence. Then she said, "Please do tell me about yourself, Mister Cannonball."

Swallowing hard, Henry worked up some voice and began to talk. At first he stammered a bit but then he got the hang of it. The words started coming out one right after another, neat as you please.

He regaled her with the entirety of the first book he'd read about The Cannonball Kid and was almost up to the place where he'd left off in the second book when she interrupted him.

"It's getting a little chilly, isn't it?"

"Er—uh—" he said, losing the thread of his narrative. "Er—uh—maybe we'd better go back to the house."

154

"Oh no! I'm only the least bit chilly." She hesitated, eyeing him expectantly.

He just stood there.

She lifted a brow at him, lowered it, then said, "Please do go on with your story, I'm dying to hear the outcome of it."

"Er—uh—" he said again. He realized suddenly that he couldn't go on much longer. He had no idea yet what the outcome might be. "Er—uh—we'd better go back. It's gonna get colder."

"But Mister Cannonball—"

"We'd better go back," he insisted.

"Only if you promise me you'll come again and tell me the rest of it." She smiled coyly at him.

He promised.

When he got back to Miz Maggie's, he took a lamp into his cubby and read until his eyes absolutely refused to stay open any longer. The next morning Miz Maggie woke him early. To his surprise she was not clutching her wrapper around her, but was already dressed. She was decked out in a plain dark riding skirt and jacket, with her hair pulled back and tied at the nape of her neck. Her face was pale and her expression almost grim. But she assured Henry he had absolutely nothing to worry about.

Taking her at her word, he began cheerily to rig himself up in the outfit Mister Hooper had given him. While he dressed, she explained that she wouldn't be able to go with him, but that the meeting with Butch Bailey had to take place in a very particular manner. She told him exactly where he should stand, and where Butch Bailey should stand. And she said very firmly that unless it was done just as she said, Henry should refuse to go through with it. She made him promise, with his hand over his heart, that he'd follow her orders precisely.

Then she sent him on his way.

The crowd that had lined Buskin's sole street yesterday was nothing compared to the mob that thronged it today. Word of the impending encounter had gone out over the telegraph. All along the line, folk had saddled up or harnessed up to hurry to Buskin. Some had even walked.

As Henry appeared, there was a wild round of applause. Several people waved flags. Some fired off guns. It was too much for Henry's horse. Nostrils flared and eyes rolling, the excited animal did a fancy fast step the entire length of the street. Pleased and impressed, the crowd increased its cheering.

The Mayor and Butch Bailey were waiting in front of The Flying Eagle Saloon. Eventually, Henry managed to maneuver the poor horse to their general vicinity. With a sigh of relief, he flung himself out of the saddle.

"Magnificent horseman," the Mayor commented.

"Damned show-off," Butch Bailey mumbled. He worked his cud and spat. He was wearing two guns slung low on his hips. He ran his thumbs along the butts and eyed Henry.

Henry grinned sociably at him.

The Mayor doffed his plug hat, intending to speak a few words before the meet. But Henry interrupted.

Eager to carry out Miz Maggie's orders, Henry took a deep breath and blurted, "Mister Mayor Sir, there's a way all this has got to be done. I got to stand there." He pointed into the street. "And Mister Bailey's got to be over there." He pointed again. "Is that all right?"

Taken aback, the Mayor looked at Butch Bailey.

156

"What the hell," Bailey said, rolling his cud to the other cheek. "I don't care where I stand. He's the one as is gonna eat dirt."

The crowd cheered.

The Mayor cleared his throat preparatory to starting his speech. But Henry was already marching off to his position, and Bailey was tromping over to his place. They turned to face each other.

The crowd pressed back against the store fronts, leaving a lot of space around the two men. Some darted behind wagons and other large objects. The Mayor gave up on his speech and stepped back into the doorway of the saloon.

"One," he said.

"Two." The crowd joined in.

"Three."

Henry grabbed for his gun. The spring loaded holster flung it into his hand. At the same instant, he saw Butch Bailey's hand all full of revolver rising to point toward him.

A shot rang out.

Bailey wavered as his pistol spat. Henry felt his own gun buck. His eyes squinched shut.

When he got them open again, he saw Bailey lying limp on the ground.

The Mayor trotted up to Henry's side and began to pound him heartily on the back. Then someone else did it too. It seemed like everybody was pressing around him then, banging him on the back or pumping his hand.

It was all very strange. He felt odd, as if he weren't really just plain Henry Caleb Lacey, Junior.

He felt as if perhaps, just possibly, he might actually be The Cannonball Kid.

CHAPTER 20

NOBODY WAS MINDING THE STORE. EVERYBODY wanted to see the showdown between The Cannonball Kid and Butch Bailey. Mister Hooper wanted to see it, too, so the General Mercantile was temporarily closed.

On the roof of the store, behind the facade of its false front, Miz Maggie watched Butch Bailey topple into the dust. Satisfied, she tucked her Winchester under her arm, pocketed the empty shell it had ejected, and scanned the roof to be sure she hadn't left any telltale signs of her presence. Then she went to the trap door and lowered herself cautiously down the ladder into the empty store. She returned the ladder to stock, ducked through the back door, and slipped the latch behind her. With a relieved sigh, she stepped up onto her horse and headed home.

By the time Henry escaped his admirers and got himself back to the house, Miz Maggie had stowed away the rifle and changed her clothes. When Henry came into the parlor, she was sitting there taking a cup of tea.

"How did it go?" she asked innocently.

"Just fine! I done it! Just like in the books, I done it!"

"Clever boy." She smiled at him. "Now you'd better give me your gun. I'll clean it for you."

"Yes, ma'am. I sure wish you'd been there, Miz Maggie. I sure wish you coulda seen it."

"I'm sure it was a sight worth seeing."

"Yes, ma'am! Can I have a drink, ma'am?"

Leaving Henry with the brandy decanter in his hand, Miz Maggie carried his revolver up to her room. She locked the door behind her. Seating herself on the bed, she emptied the cylinder of the cartridges she'd loaded in earlier. All were blanks. It seemed a wise precaution

158

for the protection of the spectators. After she hid the blanks away, she cleaned the gun.

When she took it back to Henry, she told him, "Well now, I think it's time for you to move on."

"On, ma'am?"

"Yes. You know. Get out of town."

"Oh. Er—uh—ma'am—I—uh—"

"What is it, Cannonball?"

"Ma'am, I *can't* go just now. Folks are getting up another party for me for tonight and I kinda promised I'd go to it and—uh—er—and—"

"And?"

"I kinda promised Miss Lavinia and the Mayor I'd have supper with them tomorrow night—and—and—"

"And?"

"I kinda promised somebody else for the night after that and—and—"

"And the night after that?"

"Yes, ma'am. I ain't sure, Miz Maggie, but the way I reckon it, I kinda promised every night for a week. I give my word, ma'am. I'm kinda obliged. I got to stay for a week."

"Oh, God!" Miz Maggie groaned.

Tentatively Henry suggested, "Maybe I can leave after then."

By the end of the week Henry had somehow or another made engagements for every evening for the rest of the month.

By the end of the month, hardly anybody in Buskin would even consider the possibility of The Cannonball Kid leaving town. Tourists no longer simply stopped over between trains to get a look at The Kid. Now they were coming to town especially to see him.

159

Buskin was abustle. Business was booming. All in all, the town was enjoying a prosperity nobody, except possibly the Mayor, had ever dreamed of. Townsfolk would have been loathe to lose The Cannonball Kid.

And Henry would have been loathe to go. Everybody was waving real friendly at him on the street and setting him up drinks whenever he walked into a saloon, and he was getting all the food he could eat, and Miss Lavinia smiled real pretty at him and walked out with him, and he'd never had so much fun in his life. He only wished Uncle Ned and the Professor were there to share it.

It was a day late in June when Henry woke to a throbbing like the distant thud thud of a bass drum. He hurried into his clothes, buckled on his guns and dashed out to saddle the big white horse the town had presented to him the previous week. Mounting up, he headed hopefully in search of the source of the sound.

He found the red and white wagon with the bright gilt woodwork in the field behind the railroad station. The signs on it now said *Doctor Sylvester's Marvelous Medicinal Oil* instead of *Professor Whit's Wonder Elixir,* but there was no mistaking that wagon or the befreckled man in the white frock coat who was beating the big red bass drum.

The thump thump had drawn a crowd. People pressed in all around the tailgate platform. Satisfied with the assemblage, the Professor slipped off his drum and lifted his hands for attention.

At the outer fringe of the mob, Henry dismounted. He planned on worming his way among the spectators up to the stage. But about halfway in, he found himself stalled. He was jammed up behind a pair of very large ladies in full bustles and plumed bonnets. He couldn't get past them, or around them or even see over them. On the platform, the Professor began his spiel. "Ladies and gentlemen, I'm here to say it's with the utmost pleasure that I greet you today—"

"Mister Professor!" Henry shouted. He recalled the piece of playacting Uncle Ned had done with the Professor back in Omaha. He hoped he could remember it all. "Mister Professor, sir, I been seeking for you all over to the corners of the earth!"

The Professor started. Shading his eyes with his hand, he squinted into the crowd. Puzzled, he called, "Sir? I'm afraid I'm unable to see you, sir."

Henry couldn't see the Professor either. Even on tiptoe, he could see only hat plumes. He waved a hopeful hand and hollered, "Here I am!"

People immediately around him looked at him. Some recognized him. A murmur ran through the mob. Then a spattering of shouts.

"It's The Kid!"

"The Cannonball Kid!"

"The Kid's here!"

The Professor lost his audience. The entire tip was turning away from him, trying to catch sight of the fabulous Cannonball Kid.

Henry had their attention, even that of the two beplumed matrons. Politely, he asked, "Can I please get through to the stage?"

"Make way!" someone shouted. "Everybody make way for The Cannonball Kid!"

The matrons began nudging and shoving until they had opened a space between them. Henry darted through it with a quick, "Thank you, ma'ams."

One matron smiled. The other sighed. Both agreed

that The Kid certainly was a nice mannerly boy. And handsome, too.

Ahead more people forced openings. The crowd parted to let The Cannonball Kid pass.

On the platform, the Professor anxiously awaited the emergence of the famous gunfighter. He wondered why The Cannonball Kid was seeking *him*. He hoped The Kid wanted a bottle of flukum. He feared The Kid had a pretty sister or wife in some town he'd visited in the past.

Finally Henry reached the stage. Trying hard to remember Uncle Ned's part in the playacting, he looked up at the Professor and said, "Sir, I been seeking after you all over the place."

The Professor looked down and said, "Good God, Henry!"

"Yes, sir!"

"I—they—I thought they said The Cannonball Kid—"

"Yes, sir!" Henry beamed proudly. "That's me! I'm The Cannonball Kid!"

"*You?*"

"Yes, sir!"

The Professor wiped a hand across his face. He looked at Henry. At the audience. At Henry again. With due solemnity, he held his hand out to Henry and said loudly, "Won't you step up onto the stage, sir, so everyone can see you?"

Grabbing the hand, Henry clambered up. He faced the crowd. They raised a rousing cheer.

"*You're* The Cannonball Kid?" the Professor said softly.

Henry bobbed his head and grinned.

The Professor leaned toward him and whispered, "Let me handle this."

Henry nodded.

Turning to the audience, the Professor declaimed, "Do I understand, sir, that you wish to acquire a modicum of Doctor Sylvester's Marvelous Medicinal Oil?"

"Yes, sir," Henry said.

The crowd cheered.

The Professor reached into a box sitting on the stage. He brought out a bottle. It looked exactly like a bottle of Professor Whit's Wonder Elixir. He held it toward Henry. "With my compliments, sir."

The crowd cheered again.

Accepting the bottle, Henry said, "As I recollect, I think I ought to pay you for it."

The Professor bowed slightly and answered loudly, "It is my pleasure, sir, to be of service to humanity. It is to this end that I have devoted my life. I deem it a privilege to serve such a personage as the renowned Cannonball Kid with my marvelous medicinal oil."

The crowd set up another round of cheers.

Henry licked his lips hesitantly. He whispered, "I ain't sure what I say next."

The Professor answered softly, "Insist on giving me money."

Henry brightened. He fingered a coin out of his pocket and said, "Here, Mister Professor, I insist."

"If you insist," the Professor allowed. He took the coin. It was a ten cent piece. Holding it hidden in the cup of his hand, he announced to his audience, "This is a five dollar gold piece. The price of my medicinal oil is only one dollar a bottle. I must get change for The Cannonball Kid."

"Uh—er—" Henry said.

Leaning toward him, the Professor prompted, "Tell me to take it all, money alone isn't sufficient payment for the miracle contained in this small bottle."

"Uh—er—" Henry said.

"Never mind," the Professor whispered. Looking to his audience again, he called out, "Nay, sir, I cannot take it all. Although money alone isn't sufficient payment for the miracle contained in this small bottle, I refuse to profit through the suffering of mankind. I will accept no more reimbursement per bottle than my own outlay. As I have said, it is my function to serve humanity. I make this miraculous medicinal oil available to one and all for a mere pittance. I shall not, under any circumstance, accept more than a dollar a bottle for it."

A man in the crowd waved a coin and called, "If it's good enough for The Cannonball Kid, it's sure good enough for me!"

And the rush was on.

The Professor didn't even have to make his usual offer of today-and-today-only-at-half-price. People were shoving, pushing, elbowing, and shouting for the opportunity to pay a full dollar a bottle.

Henry stood back watching while the Professor distributed flukum and collected money as fast as his hands could move. When the box of bottles was almost empty, the Professor looked toward him and said, "Henry, there's another batch made up in the wagon. Bring it to me, will you?"

"Yes sir!" Pleased to be able to help, Henry ducked behind the curtain into the wagon.

The cozy little room wasn't empty. A woman lay sprawled on the cot with a corner of a sheet barely covering a small part of her. She wasn't wearing a nightgown.

Henry froze in his tracks, his eyes wide and his mouth

164

agape. From outside, the Professor called, "Henry?"

The woman stirred. She blinked open an eye. Discovering Henry, she jerked the sheet up over her. "What the hell do you want?"

"A—er—a—" For a moment he couldn't remember. Then it came back to him. "A b-bottle of b-boxes."

She pointed a sharp finger toward a packing case in a corner.

"Henry?" the Professor called again.

Henry grabbed the box and darted back past the curtain. As he set it down at the Professor's side, he said, "Sir, there's a—a—er—a lady in your wagon."

"Of course," the Professor answered as he continued snatching money and passing flukum.

Bewildered, Henry stepped back out of his way. Bottles clattered and coins clinked. At last the final satisfied customer left clutching his precious flask of the same medicinal oil that The Cannonball Kid used.

The Professor turned to Henry and grinned. "It's good to see you again, lad. But pray tell me, what in the name of Nebuchadnezzar is this grift about *you* being The Cannonball Kid?"

"I'm awful glad to see you, too, Professor. I seen you once off a train only you was going the wrong way. Or I was. Anyway, I seen you but you didn't see me. You had a lady with you."

"Of course. But what about this Cannonball Kid business?"

"It's kinda a long story and I promised I wouldn't tell nobody except Uncle Ned only I think I said you too. I *think* I can tell you."

"Certainly you can. Come on inside and we'll discuss it in comfort." The Professor reached for the curtain. He paused and called, "Dora, are you decent?"

A disgruntled female voice answered from within the wagon, "For *you*?"

"I have a guest with me. A rather distinguished guest."

"Oh hell," the woman muttered. After a moment, she said, "All right, come on in."

The Professor lifted the curtain and gestured Henry inside.

CHAPTER 21

HESITANTLY HENRY STEPPED INTO THE WAGON.

The woman was sitting on the cot with a wrapper pulled around her. Her hair was tousled, her eyes were bleary and her feet were bare. She gave Henry a distasteful glance, thrust out her lower lip, and addressed the Professor.

"What's the big idea of sending that brat in here while I was sleeping?"

"My dear," he answered in most amiable tone. "If you would be so good as to arise at a reasonable hour and assist me in my performance, it wouldn't be necessary for me to request aid from bystanders."

Pushing her lip out ever further, she said, "Clar, you're a bastard."

He nodded. With a gesture toward Henry, he said, "Dora, my dove, I take great pleasure in presenting an old acquaintance and close friend, Henry Caleb Lacey, Junior."

Henry grinned with delight at having his whole name remembered. He doffed his Stetson and gave a little bow. "How do, ma'am."

She didn't offer her knuckles to be kissed. She didn't

even say hello. She simply sniffed disdainfully.

The Professor continued, "Perhaps Henry would be more readily known to you, my dove, as The Cannonball Kid."

"*That!*" She aimed an incredulous finger at Henry.

"That," the Professor said.

"Clar, you're not only a bastard, you're a liar, too."

"That reminds me," he said, turning to Henry. "How is Ned these days?"

"I don't know," Henry said sadly. "I ain't seen Uncle Ned for nigh a year now. He up and disappeared in San Francisco. He didn't even say goodbye."

"Oh?" The Professor looked rather surprised. "I would have thought he was the one behind this Cannonball Kid con."

"No, sir," Henry said, forcing his eyes away from the bit of white knee Dora's wrapper revealed. He felt odd. His mouth was all dry and his stomach seemed wobbly. He had a strong craving for a strong drink. "Mister Professor, sir, is that there medicine oil of yours made out of the same good drinking stuff as your wonder elixir?"

"No, the medicinal oil is most definitely for external use only. However, I do happened to have some spirits on hand for personal use. Would you care for a cup?"

"I sure would!"

The Professor took a bottle from a cupboard and set up three cups. As he poured, he told Henry, "I had to discontinue the elixir temporarily. Alcohol is its most essential ingredient and there seems to be a dearth of strong spirits in this vicinity. Even home brew is available only at outrageously exorbitant prices."

"To you everything is outrageously exorbitant," Dora muttered as she accepted the cup he offered her.

"That's on account of all the tourists," Henry said. "There's more tourists here now than there is things to sell them. The prices of everything has went way up."

The Professor nodded sadly and handed Henry a cup. He took a swallow from his own cup, then said, "It's put me into an unpleasant position. I had hoped never to concoct this particular flukum again."

"Why?" Henry asked.

"The last time I hawked this recipe, an extremely unfortunate thing happened."

"What?"

"I was vending the stuff in some obscure corner of Louisiana and an imbecile of a farmer mistakenly gave an internal dose to his horse. The medicinal oil is strictly for *external* use. I made that quite clear. But this fool fed it to his horse. A great monster of a Normandy horse. Just one tablespoon and the poor beast instantly collapsed."

"That's terrible!" Henry said sympathetically.

"Terrible, indeed!" the Professor agreed. "I didn't learn of the dolt's mistake until he and a tar barrel committee of his friends arrived at my wagon ready for action. A humiliating experience. Rather painful too. It took me weeks to get all the stuff off. I shudder at the recollection."

With something of a smirk, Dora asked him, "Feathers too?"

"Feathers too," he admitted with a sigh.

"I wish I could have seen you," she chortled.

The Professor took a long swig of whiskey and changed the subject. "Now, Henry, tell me about this business of your being The Cannonball Kid."

"You mean this pisspants little squirt really is The Cannonball Kid?" Dora said.

168

The Professor looked askance at her. "My dove, you know, you are rather a foul-mouthed slattern."

"Are you calling me names?"

"Yes, my dove."

"I got half a notion to walk out on you."

"It would be my pleasure, Dora darling."

He turned to Henry again. "You have no idea what a charming bit of feminine enchantment Dora appeared to be when first we met. The transformation that has taken place within a few short weeks is absolutely astonishing."

"A few short weeks with you is enough to shatter the illusions of any girl," Dora said. "You bastard."

The Professor sighed sadly. He commented, "Limited vocabulary. A fine body, but absolutely no intellect. No practical discretion whatsoever."

Dora said, "Never gives a girl so much as a nickel for a pretty. Not one cent on her back. She might be in rags and tatters for all he cares."

The Professor said, "A completely extravagant spendthrift slavering after every overpriced jimcrack a peddler ever packed."

Henry said, "I think I'd better go."

"Excellent idea, my lad. I'll go with you." The Professor downed the remainder of his drink and set his cup on the counter. "Perhaps we can locate some haven of privacy where we can hold a quiet conversation of masculine sensibility without these eternal outlandish disruptions. Dora, my dear, would it be too much to ask you to clean the place up while I'm out?"

"Yes!"

He shrugged. And ducked past the curtain just as she flung her cup at his head. Henry scooted out after him.

As they strolled along the street, Henry asked, "Who is she?"

"A creature of cunning who passed herself off on me as worthy of more than passing fancy, alas."

"Are you married to her?"

"Heavens no! Thank God! A wife like that could drive a man to drink." The Professor stopped suddenly. They were in front of The Flying Eagle Saloon. He sniffed the aroma of strong spirits that wafted through the doorway. "This would appear a likely retreat."

"It's a good place," Henry said, following him in.

At the sight of Henry, the saloon's customers raised a cheer. People pushed forward to ask for autographs. The bartender offered a complimentary bottle.

Henry obliged his fans with his signature and then steered the Professor to one of the small private rooms in the back. As he closed the door behind him, the Professor told him, "I am duly impressed by your reception in this establishment. If I had any doubts about you, they are vanished. Henry, you are indeed The Cannonball Kid."

"Yes, sir," Henry said. He sat down and set up the drinks.

The Professor asked him, "And you haven't heard from your errant uncle since this occurred?"

"No, sir."

"Odd. A fancier of fiction like Ned must be familiar with the literary fame of The Cannonball Kid. He can't fail to recognize the financial advantages that could be achieved through proper exploitation. I certainly hope nothing untoward has happened to the old bastard."

Henry nodded in agreement.

The Professor took a drink, then added, "I doubt Ned would have much appreciation for the accommodations at some hardrock hotel."

"Sir?"

"Your Uncle Ned isn't the type who'd take well to life behind prison bars."

"He's in *jail!*" Henry squeaked, appalled at the idea.

"In our line, it's always a possibility," the Professor allowed. "Certainly something is keeping the grubbing old grifter from showing up here to cut himself in on your con."

Henry sipped his whiskey while he thought about it. He suggested, "Maybe Uncle Ned doesn't know The Cannonball Kid is me. I didn't know it myself up till a couple of months ago."

"Oh? Then you didn't contrive it? But of course not. Tell me, Henry, just how did you come to have all this fame heaped upon your humble head?"

Henry began his story at the point where he and Uncle Ned bade farewell to the Professor in Fremont. He told it all in excess detail, from that moment until the present moment.

When he finally stopped, the Professor whistled through his teeth, then asked him, "You really did manage to outgun Butch Bailey?"

"Yes, sir!" Henry beamed and poured another round.

"How?"

"I dunno. I reckon I just got a natural knack. Seems like I got real good luck nowadays. Like how lucky it is you come to town while I'm here, Professor. I sure am glad to see you."

"My presence is hardly due to any mysterious machinations of fate. I come where the crowds are. I'm here to bring my miraculous medicinal oil to the masses of spectators who'll assemble to witness your impending affair with the notorious Whip Snade."

"Whip Snade? Who's he?"

171

The Professor cocked his head and eyed Henry. "You don't know?"

"I reckon not."

"But you—you did challenge Snade, didn't you?"

"Me?" Henry looked blank. "I don't know Mister Snade. Leastways I don't think I know him. I ain't never heard of him."

"Then I suspect there's something foul afoot," the Professor said. "A few days ago I happened to be in Cheyenne City. That's where Snade's hanging out now. I chanced to be within eavesdropping range when he received a telegram offering him a challenge to meet The Cannonball Kid here in Buskin on the Fourth of July."

"That's next week."

"Yes. Henry, if you didn't send that challenge, then who did?"

A rap sounded at the door. The voice of the town telegrapher called out "Mister Cannonball Kid, are you in there? I got a telegram for you."

"For *me*?" Henry had never received a telegram before. He'd never even seen one. The idea of having one of his own was exciting, and a little frightening. He dashed to the door and collected the sealed envelope. With trembling fingers he tore it open.

The hand scrawled message ran almost two pages. Boiled down to its essence, it said that the notorious gunfighter, Whip Snade, had issued a challenge to the famous Cannonball Kid to meet him in a public showdown in Buskin on the Fourth of July and that the world-renowned author, Colonel Buck McGunn, would be in attendance to give the event the superior literary coverage it would undoubtedly warrant.

The sender of the telegram was named as Colonel Buck McGunn.

172

Henry was awed. He touched the telegrapher's transcription of the signature as reverently as if it had actually been written by the very hand of the fabulous litterateur himself.

The Professor was enviously impressed. "A damned clever devil, this McGunn. He's dreamed up this scheme for his own profit and issued the challenges himself. He's put you and Snade into positions where neither of you can very well refuse."

"I don't mind meeting Mister Snade," Henry said. "And I sure do want to meet Mister Colonel Buck McGunn! I'll bet he's about the greatest man in the whole world! I got to run tell Miz Maggie about this!"

Clutching the precious telegram, he dashed out of the room.

Miz Maggie was taken aback.

Aghast.

Overwhelmed.

The news so upset her that she completely forgot about giving Henry his daily bath.

She wanted him to leave. She pleaded with him to get on his horse and get. She begged so desperately that he had an awful hard time saying no to her.

But he sure couldn't just up and leave without he got to see the real live Mister Colonel Buck McGunn in person, could he?

The next morning a second telegram arrived. This one was addressed not only to The Cannonball Kid but to the entire populace of Buskin, Wyoming, permanent and transient. It proclaimed that the Colonel was on his way and could be expected in town by special train shortly after noon of the following day.

The following day Buskin was a babbling bedlam of

hustle and bustle. Banners were stretched across the street, buntings hung on store fronts, welcoming signs posted about, and younguns all slicked up in their Sunday best.

Long before noon, crowds began to gather around the railroad station. While they waited, Wilson Ransom passed among them hawking picnic lunches, the proprietor of The Flying Eagle Saloon set up a portable bar, and the Professor entertained with his best lectures on the miraculous attributes of Doctor Sylvester's Marvelous Medicinal Oil.

The Mayor arrived in his claw hammer coat and a brand new silk stovepipe hat. In one hand he clutched the Key To The City Of Buskin. In the other he balanced his complete collection of the published works of Colonel Buck McGunn, which he hoped to have autographed after he'd made his welcoming speech.

Miss Lavinia, radiant in white lace with pink bows, followed after him carrying a parasol to protect her delicate complexion and a bouquet of wildflowers to present to the Colonel. Her cheeks were so rosy, her lips so bright, that several women whispered to each other that she appeared to be wearing paint.

As was befitting, Henry arrived on horseback. Despite the heat, he wore his woolen shield-front shirt and the hairy Montana chaps, as well as his white sombrero and the erstwhile Wade Desmond's sixguns. He wanted to look just the way he did on the covers of the books when he met the Colonel.

He rode escort for the carriage carrying Miz Maggie and her girls. The women were all in their finest finery. All were chattering and giggling except Miz Maggie. She sat with her hands folded in her lap and her eyes set on the far distance, looking rather solemn and pale for such a festive occasion.

Henry tied his horse and took his leave of the ladies. He hurried over to join the Mayor and Miss Lavinia. The Mayor handed him the books to hold and began rehearsing his welcoming speech. Miss Lavinia gave him a small special smile. He grinned back at her.

On the horizon a plume of smoke heralded an oncoming train.

The bandmaster arrived on horseback, at a gallop, waving a handful of papers. Assembling the band, he passed out the parts for a new original march he'd hurriedly composed in honor of Colonel Buck McGunn. Each musician anxiously started to practice his own piece.

The locomotive hove into view. It was a 2-6-0 Mogul with smoke billowing gorgeously from its diamond stack, its brass glittering in the midday sun, and the white *special* flags on its pilot whipping in the wind of its own passage. Behind the tender, it hauled a single private car.

The car was bedecked with red, white and blue bunting. On each side it carried a banner lettered in lavish scarlet and gold: *Colonel Buck McGunn.* From the observation platform there fluttered two huge American flags.

The whistle wailed as the locomotive rolled into the station.

The crowd answered with a cheer.

The band began to play the new piece, which sounded curiously like *Marching Through Georgia.*

Horses snorted and skittered. Dogs yowled. A confused rooster crowed its customary announcement of impending dawn.

The Mayor dropped The Key To The City.

Henry dropped the Mayor's books.

People shoved up all around the private car. Small boys grabbed the railing of the observation platform and pulled themselves up for a close look. As eager as any small boy, Henry forced his way to the platform, caught hold of the railing and joined them. Clinging there, he stared at the door that had just clicked and was sliding open.

The man who stepped out onto the platform was tall and well built, somewhere in his mid years. The suit he wore was dove gray, custom tailored in the most elegant fashion. His splendid beaver matched it perfectly. His black cravat was of pure Cantonese silk, set off with a stickpin bearing a single superb pearl. The gold watch chain that spanned his vest was massive.

As befit a man of letters, he wore chin whiskers. They were short and neatly trimmed, naturally dark, peppered with a most distinguished gray.

All in all, he was a remarkably fine figure of a man.

At the sight of him, Henry's jaw dropped. His eyes widened. He gasped, "Uncle Ned!"

CHAPTER 22

EDWARD JONATHAN OLDCASTLE, OR AS HE WAS NOW far better known, Colonel Buck McGunn, squinted at the youth hanging from the railing of the observation platform.

Tentatively, he said, "Nephew?"

Henry nodded. "It's me, Uncle Ned! Henry Caleb Lacey, Junior! It's me! I'm the Cannonball Kid!"

"Good God," Uncle Ned said.

The crowd cheered.

In her carriage, Miz Maggie stood up. She peered at Colonel Buck McGunn. One of the girls had brought along opera glasses. Snatching them, Miz Maggie aimed them at the Colonel. She looked through them, adjusted the focus, frowned and fainted.

Instantly the Professor leaped from the tailgate of his wagon and rushed toward her.

"Stand back! I'm a medical man!" he shouted, waving a bottle of his marvelous medicinal oil. By the time he reached Miz Maggie's side, she was reviving. He barely got the cork out of the bottle when she opened her eyes. He thrust the bottle quickly under her nose.

She sniffed, sneezed and shoved it away.

The Professor addressed the crowd. "The Dear Lady is recovering, thanks to the unparalleled curative powers of just one single whiff of Doctor Sylvester's Marvelous Medicinal Oil!"

Struggling through the assemblage, the Mayor arrived at the observation platform. Ready to proceed with his speech, he gestured for attention. The bandmaster, mistaking the meaning of the motions, signaled for the band to play. It struck up the new march again.

Cheering spectators surged onto the observation platform. Men grabbed the Colonel. More men grabbed Henry. In a moment, both were perched atop husky shoulders, bobbing above a sea of admirers.

The Mayor saw his entire audience rushing away from him. He tried to call them back, but it was futile. Finally he gave up and followed.

The crowd filled Buskin's street and overflowed into its saloons. For all practical purposes the party in honor of Colonel Buck McGunn had begun.

When Henry was finally let down from the shoulders of his fans, he couldn't locate Uncle Ned at all. In fact, he could hardly move. Sweating and panting, he stood in the midst of the mob. People milled around him, thrusting pens and paper at him, or grabbing his hand to pump it, or slapping him on the back.

By twilight, he still hadn't managed to make contact with his uncle. His hand ached, his fingers were numb, and his back was so sore he winced at a touch. And he wanted something awful to get into some cooler clothes. He stopped thinking about finding Uncle Ned and began to concentrate on hopes of escape.

Someone pushed a pencil into his hand and held a copy of one of the books toward him. As he reached to sign it, his sweat-slick fingers let the pencil slip away. He hunkered to search for it. He couldn't find it. When he tried to rise, he discovered the gap above him had closed. As people all around asked each other what had become of The Kid, he took the opportunity to slither off on his hands and knees.

He emerged from the forest of legs not far from the railroad station. Across the tracks he could see the Professor's wagon.

Despite the growing darkness, the torches on the tailgate weren't lit. The big bass drum lay on its side next to a box of bottles. The Professor himself sat on the edge of the stage, his legs dangling. He sipped from a cup of whiskey as he watched the festivities up the street.

Henry waved and dashed toward him.

"Hullo, Henry," he said rather quietly.

"Professor! Professor, sir!" Henry gasped. "That's my Uncle Ned! Mister Colonel Buck McGunn is my own Uncle Ned!"

178

"A remarkable man," the Professor observed. "I knew he'd go far once he found his proper field of endeavor. But it never occurred to me he'd become a distinguished master of letters. I wonder if perhaps I should try my own hand at the literary arts."

"I want to see him but I can't find him. There won't nobody let me be. They keep making me write my name and push me and shove me and I can't find him."

"Patience, Henry. You'll see him in time. But for the moment, he belongs to the world. Come on inside. You'll be safe from your admirers there."

The Professor got to his feet. He glanced at his equipment, looked enviously toward the distant crowd, sighed, then led Henry into the wagon. Inside, he lit a small lamp. He poured Henry a drink and refreshed his own.

Taking the cup, Henry asked, "How come you're not selling your medicine? There's a real swell crowd now."

"Indeed there is. But alas, the heroes of the day have the entire attention of the assemblage. I tried my pitch and couldn't attract as much as a dozen vile urchins away from you and Ned." The Professor sighed again. "Perhaps later, when the novelty wears off a bit, they'll be willing to heed the state of their health. For now, patience."

He sat down on the cot and sipped his drink.

Henry unbuttoned his shirt, skinned out of his chaps, and settled comfortably on the crate in the corner. The lamp filled the wagon with a cozy glow. It was pleasantly quiet. Very pleasant just to sit and sip whiskey in silence.

Suddenly it occurred to Henry that something was amiss. He asked. "Where's Miss Dora?"

"She was gracious enough to desert me," the

Professor answered. He rose to refresh his drink. "And ungracious enough to take the twenty dollars I had hidden among the coffee beans. Thank God she never knew where the rest is cached. The bitch. Is money the only thing that can really hold a woman's heart? Here, Henry, another drink will cheer you up."

As he refilled Henry's cup, he added, "Speaking of women, are you perchance acquainted with a most attractive young thing called Sally? She would seem to be in residence at the household where you presently make your abode."

"Miss Sally? Sure. She's real nice. She's the one who made up that song about me."

"Ah, a creature of artistic attainment as well as physical attraction. A rare combination. Hullo? Did you hear something?"

Henry shook his head.

The Professor frowned slightly, listening.

There was a scraping noise near the back of the wagon. Then a surreptitious knock at the tailgate.

The Professor called, "Come on in."

Uncle Ned came on in. He looked a far cry from the fine figure he'd cut on his arrival. He had lost his hat, his cravat, and his collar stud. The stiff linen collar stuck out from his neck, held in place only by its back button. His hair was mussed, his clothes were disheveled, and one coat sleeve was half torn off.

With unspoken sympathy, the Professor poured an additional cup of whiskey and held it out to him.

He grabbed it, downed it, then sighed deeply and said hoarsely, "Thank God!"

"Thank *me*," the Professor said. "It's *my* whiskey. How did you get away from them, Ned?"

"I knocked a plank out of the back wall of an

outhouse and slipped away through the opening." Uncle Ned plopped himself on the cot and sunk his chin into his hands. He mumbled. "Fame has its drawbacks. Please pour me another, Clarence, old friend."

"Hello, Uncle Ned." Henry ventured rather shyly from his corner. "I'm awful glad to see you again."

Uncle Ned lifted his head just enough to look at his nephew. "My boy, my boy, you have no idea of the extent to which it gladdens these weary orbs to again behold your bright and cherubic countenance."

"Sir?"

"He's glad to see you, too," the Professor said, handing Uncle Ned a fresh drink.

"However," Uncle Ned continued. He paused for a long swallow of whiskey. "However, I can think of little that would so astonish and appall me as the revelation that my own dear youthful ward should have become the notorious Cannonball Kid during my brief absence."

The Professor lifted a skeptical brow. "*Appall* you, Ned? When there's such opportunity for profit in it?"

"At the boy's peril?" Uncle Ned cocked a scornful brow back at him.

"How come you left me, Uncle Ned?" Henry asked. "How come you run off and left me in San Francisco and didn't even say goodbye to me or nothing?"

"Yes, Ned. That seems the act of a scoundrel," the Professor said.

"Alas!" Uncle Ned sighed. "It was none of my own intention. As it happened, I dropped into the arms of Morpheus in the parlor of a house belonging to one Madame Nellie Festus. You know her, don't you, Clarence?"

"I do. And please stop calling me Clarence."

"As I said, I dropped into the arms of Morpheus in

181

her parlor and was aroused rather abruptly in the fo'c'sle of a China-bound clipper under the command of a most contemptible old goat named Horne who refused to set me ashore."

"You were shanghaied!" The Professor seemed delighted.

Morosely, Uncle Ned nodded. "Shipped aboard as a common seaman. Imagine *me*, condemned to clambering about in the rigging like a beastly monkey. The indignity of it!"

The Professor laughed.

"Did you go to China, sir?" Henry asked.

"No. By great good fortune I was able to jump ship in the Sandwich Islands and obtain return passage to Oregon aboard a Russian brig. By the time I made my way to San Francisco again, boy, you were gone. Supposedly back to that quaint village in Missouri. Indeed, I had assumed you safely ensconced among the friends of your childhood. Now I find you here in the western wilderness, dripping with revolvers, sporting a reputation as a formidable gunman. Clarence, another potation, please, while the lad explains his situation."

"Now that you're such a figure of affluence," the Professor said as he poured, "I trust you'll have the generous courtesy to present me with a few bottles in appreciation of all the stock you've consumed under my roof."

Ignoring him, Uncle Ned started, "Now boy, please be so good as to—"

He was interrupted by a soft knock at the back of the wagon.

"Who could that be?" the Professor muttered. He called out, "Who is it?"

The voice that replied was female. "Doctor Sylvester? I'm a customer."

"Indeed?" The Professor glanced at Uncle Ned. Uncle Ned nodded. Smiling, the Professor stepped outside.

Henry started to speak. Uncle Ned shushed him and cocked an ear. From beyond the curtain, voices were audible.

The Professor was saying, "You are Miss Sally, are you not?"

"Oh?" the girl said. "You know who I am?"

"How could any man of any degree of sensibility be in Buskin for a period of time and not become aware of the identity of such a charming lady as yourself, Miss Sally? May I ask what good fortune brings you to grace the environs of my humble caravan this lovely evening?"

"I want to get a bottle of your marvelous oil, Doctor Sylvester."

"My pleasure, my lady. I have a fresh stock in the wagon." The Professor raised his voice, as if to be certain Uncle Ned and Henry could hear him. "If you'll just step inside, I'll get you a bottle. And instruct you in its proper application."

"Then it's not for the sicknesses of the insides?" She sounded disappointed.

"Oh yes indeed it is," the Professor assured her. "For a specific ailment it should be applied over the specifically ailing member. For a general debility one applies it generally."

He raised his voice again. "If you will just accompany me into my sanctum, Miss Sally, I will most gladly and agreeably administer the marvelous oil for you."

Inside the wagon, Uncle Ned gulped down the last of his drink and started for the curtain that hung be-

183

hind the driver's seat. He gestured for Henry to come with him.

Outside, Miss Sally was saying, "It's not for me."

"Makes no difference, my dear," the Professor said. "Just step inside and I shall demonstrate the proper manner of application so that you can correctly advise the recipient of the marvelous oil."

Inside, Uncle Ned paused halfway through the front exit and gestured again for Henry to come along.

"I want you to see Miss Sally," Henry told him.

"No no, not now," he answered in a hurried whisper. "You can see her later. Come on along, boy."

Henry shook his head and stood his ground. "I want to see her now."

Outside, the Professor gave Miss Sally a hand up onto the tailgate and drew back the curtain to escort her inside. He started at the sight of Uncle Ned and Henry still on the premises. He shot them each an irate scowl, then blanked his face and said, "Hullo, are you gentlemen still here? I thought you had to leave on pressing business immediately."

"We are leaving," Uncle Ned said apologetically. "Right now."

Henry nodded in greeting to Miss Sally and said,

"Ma'am, I wanted to ask you about Miz Maggie. Is she all right? I didn't get no chance to see her after she took sick at the railroad station."

"She fainted," Miss Sally told him. "She said it was the heat and the excitement and all, but I think she's really sick. She said for us girls to take the night off, and she went straight home. And she's never done anything like that before."

Turning to the Professor, she said, "Doctor Sylvester, your medicine helped her so quick at the station, I thought it might do her good to have a whole bottle."

"She shall have a whole bottle, my dear. She shall have a dozen bottles, if you wish it, all at only half price. She shall have whatever your kind heart desires for her," the Professor said expansively.

Miss Sally giggled.

The Professor glowered at Uncle Ned and Henry. "Goodnight, gentlemen."

"But—" Henry started.

"*Goodnight!*" the Professor insisted.

Uncle Ned bobbed his head in a polite farewell to Miss Sally and scrambled on through the front exit. Reluctantly, Henry followed him.

Outside, they stopped and looked at the party that was still going full swing on the street. It seemed to have spread to Uncle Ned's private car. The windows were all aglow. Crowds of people were visible through them. Sounds of laughter, chatter, clanking glasses and a clattering banjo wafted from them.

"Oh God!" Uncle Ned groaned at the sight. "I *cannot* face that ravening horde again tonight!"

"Why don't you come back to the house with me?" Henry suggested. "I'd sure like you to meet Miz Maggie.

"The house? Who is this Miz Maggie?"

"She keeps this real nice house where Miss Sally and some other girls live. I stay there with her. She puts me kinda in mind of Madame Nellie."

"Indeed? You stay with her, you say? Indeed!"

CHAPTER 23

FOR THE FIRST TIME SINCE ITS ERECTION, THE RED-PANED lantern in front of Miz Maggie's house failed to function as a beacon for lonely wanderers in the night. Silent and dark but for a single low-turned lamp in the parlor, the house seemed mournfully forlorn.

Inside Miz Maggie sat alone, a glass in her hand and the brandy decanter at her side. She flinched at the sound of steps on the porch. As the doorlatch clicked, she started to rise. She resented the prospect of an intrusion. She was prepared to tell whoever entered that he was not welcome this night.

It was Henry who came bursting into the house, waving his hands excitedly. "Miz Maggie!" he shouted. "You got to meet my Uncle Ned!"

The renowned Colonel Buck McGunn followed him into the parlor.

Miz Maggie gazed at Uncle Ned. Slowly, she said, "Neddy?"

He cocked his head and looked at her in question. "Margaret?"

She held a hand toward him. Taking it, he pressed his lips to her knuckles, then said, "Margaret, my dear!"

She turned to Henry. "Why the devil didn't you tell me this confounded Uncle Ned of yours is Neddy Oldcastle?"

Before Henry could reply, she was addressing Uncle Ned again. "It's been a long time."

"Far too long. My dear, you are as radiant, as gloriously lovely as ever."

"And you're as honey tongued as ever, you rogue.

Good God, Ned, sit down. Have a drink. Tell me, what on earth became of you?"

Uncle Ned helped himself to a brandy.

Henry asked, "You all already know each other?"

"Your dear uncle is the charming rascal who many years ago induced me into the full flowering of my womanhood," Miz Maggie answered. "And then abandoned me."

"My dear," Uncle Ned said as he seated himself. "Can you ever forgive me?"

"Forgive you for what? For running out on me? I know now that was inevitable. For stealing me away from my family hearth and home? Poor Neddy." She smiled at him. "I am eternally indebted to you. If you had never led me into the world beyond that small circle of family and friends, I most likely would have ended up married to Charles Whateverhisnamewas that Papa had picked for me—"

"That beastly prig," Uncle Ned commented.

"—and spent my life as a common kitchen drudge changing filthy linen on squawling infants year after year. Neddy, you saved me from a fate worse then death."

"My dear!" Uncle Ned said with a modest smile. He took a swig of brandy, and went on. "My dear, I should never have left you so suddenly if it hadn't been for that totally unreasonable Papa of yours. When I heard he was on hand with both a horsewhip and a shotgun, I felt it expedient to make a hasty departure. However, I sought you again later—"

"Liar."

"I swear it, my dear. I returned but, alas, you had departed. I sought you. I have sought you all these years, to the very ends of the earth!"

"Of course you have."

"Honestly, Margaret, I did go back for you, but you were gone. I was informed you'd left with some scalawag of a ladies undergarment drummer from St. Louis."

She lifted a brow at him. "How could you know that? Unless you actually did go back for me."

"I did, my dear. Honestly, I did." She smiled at him. Tenderly, she said, "Neddy!"

"Margaret!" he said.

They looked at each other.

Suddenly Miz Maggie said, "Neddy, dear, what you need is a bath."

"A bath?"

"Upstairs. In my room."

"Ah yes! Of course! A bath!"

"Henry, fetch the tub up to my room and fill it."

"Yes Ma'am," Henry said rather reluctantly. "Do I have to take a bath too?"

"No," she told him. "Once you've filled the tub just go away. Leave the house. Go wherever you want, but go away and don't come back until tomorrow."

The night had turned chill. The vast crystal sky was spattered with stars like white ice chips. Small winds whispered in the brush.

As he walked toward town, Henry could see the bright glare of lanterns and hear the music, the laughter, of the party. It all seemed oddly alien to him. He walked in another world, a cold empty world. Uncle Ned and Miz Maggie had sent him away from the warmth of their company into the darkness.

He knew he'd be welcome at the party. He was one of the guests of honor. People would greet him, give him drinks, cheer for him.

But he didn't think they'd cheer him up at all. He couldn't stand the thought of facing all those admirers again now.

He decided he'd much rather sit quietly and sip whiskey and talk with the Professor.

But when he reached it, the Professor's wagon looked deserted. Not a whisper of light showed at the shuttered windows. Morosely he walked around it, remembering all the fun he'd had in the company of the Professor and Uncle Ned back in Omaha.

Suddenly he started. He thought he'd heard a sound from within the wagon. He leaned an ear against its wall. Yes, there were sounds within. He was certain of it.

Hopefully, he knocked at the tailgate.

There was no answer.

He knocked again, louder this time. Still he got no answer.

The third time he banged at the tailgate, the Professor's disgruntled voice called from inside, "Go away!"

"It's me, Mister Professor!" Henry shouted back.

"Goddammit, Henry, *go away*, I said!"

Henry sighed. Shoving his hands into his pockets, he walked off.

The night seemed to have gotten even colder, the nearby party even more repulsive. Head hung, he drifted toward it. He stopped outside the glare of the lights. He knew he just couldn't smile at people and sign autographs and shake hands any more tonight.

All he wanted was a quiet drink and the company of a friend.

But it appeared that none of his friends wanted his company.

He stood there in the shadows watching the dancers, sniffing the whiskey, hearing the gaiety of the music and laughter, sinking lower and lower in his own mind.

Suddenly something touched his arm.

Whirling, he found Miss Lavinia at his side. The starlight was bright in her eyes as she looked into his face.

She smiled. "Mister Cannonball, where ever have you been?"

"I dunno," he mumbled.

She asked, "Where are you going?"

"I dunno."

"Everybody's been looking for you."

"Unh," he said dully.

"You seem sad."

"Unh."

"Don't you like the party?"

"I guess I just ain't much in the mood for partying right now."

"Oh? Well, it isn't a very good party. Not without you there."

"It ain't?"

She smiled again. "It's a lovely night, isn't it?"

He glanced up at the icy sky. "I reckon."

"It would be an awfully nice night for a walk."

"I reckon it would," he agreed.

The pressure of her hand on his arm increased. He could feel the warmth of her touch. It seemed to be spreading like the heat of strong spirits. It rushed through his whole body, washing away the chill of the evening. And washing away his thoughts of Uncle Ned and the Professor.

He said, "Miss Lavinia, would you like to go for a walk?"

"Why, Mister Cannonball, how nice of you to ask!"

Her hand slid along his arm. It slipped into his. Her fingers intertwined with his.

Together they strolled into the night.

CHAPTER 24

TIME WAS SHORT. EXCEEDINGLY SHORT. WHIP SNADE was due in Buskin on July Third.

Tomorrow.

Miz Maggie was distraught. Over breakfast in bed, she discussed the situation with Uncle Ned. He assured her he'd think of something. He promised it so sincerely that she almost believed him.

All through the day, he thought.

By the following morning he had an idea. He confided it to her. Hopefully, she agreed that it just might work.

Enthusiastically, he informed her that it most certainly would work.

Somewhat cheered, she adorned herself for the trip to the station to meet the train from Cheyenne.

Henry wanted to join the welcoming committee but Uncle Ned insisted it was against every civilized Code Duello for principals to socialize prior to the main event. So while the crowds assembled at the station to watch Whip Snade arrive, Henry waited hidden in the Professor's wagon. To his delight, Miss Lavinia located him there and offered to keep him company.

At trackside, the Mayor rehearsed his speech at Uncle Ned and Miz Maggie while the band rehearsed a new original march composed by the bandmaster especially for the occasion, and the Professor entertained the

191

assemblage with his pitch. Emphasizing the value of his oil in the treatment of sore feet and sunburn, he did a brisk business.

The warning wail of a locomotive interrupted the various activities. All eyes turned to peer at the oncoming train. Hand in hand, Miss Lavinia and Henry peeked out of the wagon.

The locomotive wheezed to a halt. A mass of tourists spewed out of the cars to swell the ranks of spectators.

Then Whip Snade made his appearance.

He was a stocky man of medium height with long blond hair and a somewhat scraggly moustache. At first glance he looked rather like a drummer in his checked suit and brown bowler. At second glance, one discerned the tips of twin holsters protruding from beneath the bulging skirts of his coat. Both were lashed by thongs to his thighs.

His eyes were icy blue. Under the fringe of his moustache, his mouth was thin and hard. He stopped on the step down from the car and looked warily at the crowd.

A cheer went up.

The Mayor held out a welcoming hand and said, "Mister Whip Snade!"

Snade ignored the hand. Curling his lip, he said, "What the hell's all this ruckus?"

Uncle Ned answered him. "Your admirers, sir, come to welcome you to Buskin."

Snade scanned the crowd. A corner of his mouth twitched, signifying pleasure. Clasping his hands, he held them above his head in salute to his audience.

The crowd cheered again.

The Mayor started his speech.

"Skip it," Snade growled at him. "Is there a fit place

for a man to feed hisself in this dump?"

"Uh—why—yes," the Mayor said. "Ransom's is excellent."

"Where's it at?"

"I would be most honored to conduct you to the establishment," Uncle Ned said graciously.

Snade looked him up and down. "Who the hell are you?"

"Colonel Buck McGunn, author of the world-famous Cannonball Kid books, at your service."

"After tomorrow you're gonna have to find somebody else to write your books about."

"Should you be victorious in the impending encounter, sir," Uncle Ned told him. "I shall undoubtedly turn my talented pen to the delineation of your heroic exploits."

"You'll write about me, huh?" Snade's mouth twitched with pleasure again. He looked at Miz Maggie. Giving a jerk of his head toward her, he asked, "Who's she?"

Uncle Ned bowed slightly as he said, "Margaret, my dear, I take pleasure in presenting the famous Mister Whip Snade."

"Mister Snade, how nice," Miz Maggie said sweetly.

Snade said, "Are you at my service too?"

Uncle Ned's nostrils flared. He drew a quick breath and said rather stiffly, "I believe you were inquiring about an eating establishment, sir."

"Well, you ain't no spring chicken," Snade told Miz Maggie. He turned to Uncle Ned. "Yeah, I'm hungry."

"Then follow me, please."

Elbowing the Mayor out of the way, Snade stepped to Uncle Ned's side. Miz Maggie swung around to the other side and slipped her arm through Uncle Ned's.

A somewhat subdued crowd opened way for them.

193

They proceeded to Ransom's. Ransom dashed ahead, greeted them at the door and showed them to a table.

As he seated himself, Snade said, "Let's start with oysters and champagne."

"We—uh—I regret we're out of champagne," Ransom advised him. "And oysters aren't in season now."

"The hell you say!"

"Yes, sir."

"Dammit, I got my mouth all set for oysters and champagne. What the hell kind of a crummy dump is this, anyhow?"

Ransom winced. Rather dourly, he suggested, "I have some superb claret and all the prairie oysters you can eat."

"Hell, I've et my fill of balls when I was a punk kid riding herd," Snade grumbled. "Now I've growed up and got me some class, I don't settle for nothing but the best. What's the best you got?"

"The specialty of the house is beefsteak."

"I'm real particular what I put inside me. Only way I'll touch a beefsteak is if it's done just right."

"My restaurant is famous across the nation for its beefsteak," Ransom said proudly.

"I want it just exactly this thick," Snade measured air with thumb and forefinger. "I want a brown crust on the fat, but not no mess of burnt stuff. You understand me? I want the outside seared and the inside nigh raw. It's got to be warm clear through the middle, but not cooked none. And both sides got to be exactly the same. Don't put no fistful of salt on it neither. A pinch. Just a pinch of salt and a little shake of black pepper. You understand me?"

"Yes sir!" Ransom beamed. It was seldom he had a

194

customer who really appreciated excellent cuisine. He was certain that his well-paid chef could comply precisely with this gourmet's specific requirements.

"And plenty of ketchup," Snade added. "You got ketchup, ain't you?"

"Yes, sir," Ransom replied, drooping.

"Margaret and I shall have the same," Uncle Ned said. "However, omitting the ketchup."

"What's the matter? Don't you like ketchup?" Snade snapped at him.

"I fear I have a mild aversion to it," he said.

"Makes you sick?"

"Indeed."

Ransom shuffled off to the kitchen. He delivered the order to the cook just as Snade had given it. The cook busied himself with the craftsmanlike production of three perfect beefsteaks.

With mixed feelings, Ransom delivered the steaks to the table.

Snade took one look at his and pronounced it overdone. He told Ransom to take it back and try again. Ransom returned it to the kitchen. He slid it onto a different dish, waited a while, then took it to Snade again.

"The damn thing's raw!" Snade announced. "Can't you cook a goddamned steak around here at all!"

"If you will be so kind as to allow it, sir, I'll have the chef try again," Ransom said, mocking an air of contrition.

"Ugh," Snade replied in the affirmative.

Ransom carried the steak to the kitchen, removed it to a third plate, discussed the matter a few moments with the cook, then returned the cooling meat to Snade.

Snade studied over it. He flopped it on the plate, peering closely at each side. With the tip of his knife he flicked an imaginary bit of debris from it.

At last, he announced, "It's a hell of a lousy job of cooking a steak, but I expect it's the best you can do in a dump like this."

"Thank you, sir," Ransom said, handing him the ketchup.

"Damned dumb dumps always passing their garbage off on a man as food," Snade grumbled. He cut into the steak, took a cube of it on the knife and held it up. "Hell of a thing for a man to put into his insides."

Stuffing it into his mouth he began to chew. He ate noisily but wordlessly.

Uncle Ned made a few attempts at polite conversation. Snade's replies were simply grunts. The conversation lapsed.

When the meal was done, Snade belched, muttered something about nature, then grinned at Miz Maggie. "You wanna come along with me, Honey?"

She glared at him.

He shrugged and stalked off toward the outhouse.

As soon as he was gone, Miz Maggie leaned toward Uncle Ned and asked in an anxious whisper, "What do you think, Neddy dear? Will it work?"

"Most certainly, my dear," he said. "The creature is a completely uncivilized swine. He'll undoubtedly indulge himself intemperately in whatever is offered to him. I shall have no difficulty in, as the saying goes, drinking him under the table. By the morrow, he will be totally incapacitated. He will waken suffering the shuddering shakes, appalled at the mere sight of daylight, and aghast at any thought of actual physical endeavor whatever. He will be in no condition to succeed in a contest of speed and skill."

"You sound thoroughly familiar with the phenomenon," Miz Maggie commented.

"I am, my dear. I have observed it often in sundry unfortunate acquaintances. Harken! He's returning."

Snade strode back to the table. Slapping himself on the belly, he belched again, then asked Uncle Ned, "Where do you go to have some fun in this Godforsaken dump?"

"There are festivities planned in your honor for this evening," Uncle Ned told him.

"Festivities?" He pronounced the word as if it had an unpleasant flavor. "I hope you don't mean a bunch of old biddies doing Virginia reels and serving fruit punch?"

"Heavens no!" Uncle Ned made a face. "I can assure you the festive beverages are hearty and the company most attractive. Perhaps you'd care to sample the wares of a few local establishments prior to the commencement of the evening's activities?"

"If you're saying do I want a drink, I sure as hell do."

"I recommend The Flying Eagle for a start."

"Is that a place or a brand?"

"It is an exceedingly pleasing saloon."

"Good!" Snade looked to Miz Maggie. "You coming, honey?"

"I'm afraid I have a previous engagement," she replied.

Snade shrugged. "Well, you ain't exactly no spring chicken. I like my meat tender. Come on, Colonel, show me this saloon."

CHAPTER 25

AS THE SUN SLOWLY SETTLED ITSELF BEHIND THE horizon, the party in honor of the notorious Whip Snade officially began.

Up the street, in front of the church, Buskin's matrons smiled as they doled out fruit punch and admired the stately grace of the Virginia reel.

Down the street, near the saloons, folks laughed and chattered as the whiskey flowed, fiddles squawled, banjos jangled and square dancers bounced through their do-si-dos.

Upon Miss Sally's arrival, the Professor had ousted Miss Lavinia and Henry from the privacy of his wagon. Dutifully, they'd gone on to the party. They danced a few sets of squares, Henry signed autographs, they went once through the Virginia reel, then they disappeared. In the pleasant quiet behind the church, they strolled hand in hand into the privacy of the coming night.

Over by the railroad station, at the far end of Colonel Buck McGunn's private car, apart from all the activity, Miz Maggie sat alone in her carriage. She gazed toward the lampglow and the noisy throng that filled the street. Anxiously she awaited word from Uncle Ned.

For the folk frolicking in the street, time passed with heedless speed. For Miz Maggie it barely oozed by.

Despite the awful tension, she almost dozed. She started abruptly as she saw a curious figure detach itself from the mob. It was heading directly toward her. Silhouetted by the glow of the party lamps, it appeared to be a man bearing a cumbersome burden over his shoulder.

"Neddy?" she called softly as it approached her.

"Lady? You there?" The harsh voice that answered was by no means Uncle Ned's.

Coming up to the carriage, Whip Snade said, "They told me you was parked back here. Hell of a place to be. You want this?"

"What on earth?" she squeaked.

"Damned old ass can't hold his likker," Snade explained. He dumped the bundle from his shoulder into the carriage. "What about it, honey? Ain't you lonesome back here by yourself?"

Looking down at the limp form of Uncle Ned, Miz Maggie sighed, "Oh Neddy!

Snade shrugged. "Well, you ain't no spring chicken," he muttered as he ambled back toward the festivities.

"Go away!" the Professor howled from within the darkened wagon. "Goddammit, go away!"

Miz Maggie knocked again on the open tailgate platform, using a rock for emphasis. She called, "I *thought* you were their friend! I *thought* you cared about them! I *thought* you'd be willing to help dear Neddy save poor Cannonball's life!"

"Oh, hell," the Professor groaned. "Just a minute."

When he ducked from behind the curtain that closed off the interior of the wagon, he was still tucking in his shirttails. Slipping a suspender over one shoulder, he said, "What the devil is it? Pardon my language, madam, but you've interrupted me at rather an inconvenient moment. I sincerely hope the situation is no less dire than you imply."

"It's dire all right," Miz Maggie assured him.

He tugged the other suspender into place, then jumped down from the tailgate and said, "What would

199

seem to be the difficulty and in what manner do you feel I might be of assistance?"

"You know that poor dear little Cannonball can't possibly survive the showdown tomorrow without some kind of help."

"He said he outshot Butch Bailey. If he could do that, he's got a very good chance against Snade."

"It wasn't exactly Cannonball who shot Bailey," Miz Maggie confided.

"Ah ha! Connivance! I should have realized as much. But in that case, who did shoot Bailey?"

"I did. From hiding. But there's no way I can contrive to pull the same trick tomorrow. And even under, the best of circumstances, poor Cannonball can't hit the side of the stable."

"Then he *is* in serious danger."

"He is. Neddy had a plan but it hasn't worked."

"A plan?"

She nodded. "He meant to get this Whip Snade so thoroughly roostered tonight that Snade would be totally incapacitated tomorrow. But it hasn't worked out that way at all."

"Dear old Neddy is the one who's incapacitated, eh?"

She nodded again.

"He always did overestimate his capacity," the Professor said. He drew a deep breath. "I suppose in behalf of my dear old friend, I must brace myself and step into the breach. If Snade's half roostered now, it shouldn't be too difficult to finish the job."

"Hurry!" Miz Maggie said eagerly.

The Professor climbed back into the wagon. A murmur of voices drifted from within. When he reappeared, he was fully dressed. Doffing his white silk plug hat, he bowed to Miz Maggie.

"It is a far, far better thing I do than I have ever done—"

"Please hurry," she told him.

"The game's afoot!" he quoted dramatically as he replaced the hat on his head. Trotting off toward the festivities, he continued to himself, "Follow your spirit, and upon this charge Cry 'God for Harry, England—and dear old Neddy!' "

Uncle Ned sat with his head slumped into his hands. Occasionally he groaned.

Beside him in the carriage, Miz Maggie watched and waited in anxious silence.

A curious silhouette appeared against the glow of the lamplight in the street. It proceeded toward the carriage.

"Professor?" Miz Maggie called hopefully.

Uncle Ned groaned.

"Lady?" the voice of Whip Snade answered. "You want this one, too?"

He dumped his burden into the carriage. As he ambled back to the party, he was grumbling, "None of these jackasses around here can hold their likker."

"Professor . . . !" Miz Maggie said sadly to the form at her feet.

Uncle Ned groaned.

Cool damp cloths, hot black coffee and a little hair of the dog seemed in order. Miz Maggie went to the Professor's wagon in search of them. Miss Sally helped her carry them back to the carriage.

Miss Sally's soft hands and tender words brought the Professor around. With Miz Maggie's help, she got him sitting up with his head slumped into his hands. She wrung out a rag in cool water and pressed it to the back of his neck, then tickled his ear. He groaned.

Weakly, Uncle Ned said, "I suspect we have been barking up a blind alley. Snade seems to have an infinite capacity to absorb strong spirits."

"Bottle after bottle of Blackjack," the Professor mumbled through his fingers. "Downed like sarsaparilla, and not a sign of effect. And *I* was buying . . ."

"He has to have a weakness," Miz Maggie said. "Every man has at least one."

Miss Sally spoke up. "My mother always told me every man has three weaknesses. Gambling, strong drink, and women."

A slow smile spread itself across Miz Maggie's face. She said, "Sally, go round up all the girls. Tell them to hurry back to the house and get ready for work. Tell them to bring Snade with them. No other company, mind you. Just Snade."

"*All* of us?" Miss Sally asked.

Miz Maggie nodded.

"Ah ha," the Professor sighed with a trace of envy.

Uncle Ned agreed, "Indeed!"

For a second time, the red lantern in front of Miz Maggie's house spent the night unlit. Again, the establishment was closed to the public.

Peeking into the parlor, the morning sun found Miz Maggie slumped deep in a love seat. Beside her, Uncle Ned drowsed with his head on her shoulder. Curled on another love seat, the Professor emitted soft snortling snores.

At a sound on the stairs, Miz Maggie stirred. Uncle Ned blinked open his eyes. Both looked toward the entryway.

Whip Snade strode down the stairs and stepped into

the parlor. His hair was tousled, his moustache was disarrayed, and his shirt tails hung loose. Heartily, he announced, "Next!"

With a soulful sigh, Miz Maggie said, "There aren't any more."

Snade's mouth twitched in disappointment. "Hell, I was just getting going good."

Miz Maggie began, "Suppose *I*—"

"No, my dear," Uncle Ned whispered into her ear. "Don't sully yourself. It's no use. This creature is insatiable."

Miz Maggie sighed again, in agreement.

"How about a drink, Mister Snade?" Uncle Ned suggested.

Snade nodded. "Obliged, Colonel. Just a short one. I got me a man to kill this afternoon. If you can rightly call it a *man*."

Miz Maggie made a small strangling noise.

Uncle Ned got himself to his feet and staggered to the sideboard. He poured three fingers of whiskey into each of two glasses. One, he topped off with water, the other with sulphate of morphine. Taking care as to which was which, he handed one to Snade and kept the other for himself.

Snade emptied the mixture of whiskey and mickey in one long chug. He smacked his lips, held out the glass, and said, "Maybe just another short one."

Uncle Ned refilled the glass with the last of the whiskey and the last of the drug.

Snade emptied it. He belched and slapped himself on the stomach. "Well, if there ain't nothing else here, I'll go see what I can find me. Got all morning to kill yet."

Once he was gone, Miz Maggie looked to Uncle Ned. "What on earth can we do?"

"I don't know. I really don't know. Perhaps the mickey will eventually take effect. If not, I'll think of something. Meanwhile, my dear, would you care to accompany me upstairs?"

"Dear Neddy, you always—what was that?"

The front door crept cautiously open. Boots in hand, Henry came tiptoeing into the entryway.

"Cannonball!" Miz Maggie called to him. "Where ever have you been?"

He slunk shyly into the parlor. "I was to the party, ma'am."

"Until this hour?"

He nodded. "I'm kinda tired. I thought I might ought to get some sleep before I meet Mister Snade."

"Indeed," Uncle Ned agreed.

"Poor boy," Miz Maggie said. "You'll need all the rest you can get. Go upstairs. Use my bed."

"Margaret!" Uncle Ned exclaimed.

"Neddy dear, we must all make sacrifices."

"But—"

"Thank you, ma'am," Henry mumbled. He added his goodnights, yawned, and plodded on up the stairs.

"Poor child," Miz Maggie said as she watched him go.

Then she turned and looked at Uncle Ned.

He looked at her.

"Neddy dear," she said thoughtfully. "The girls are occupying the upstairs beds now, but there is a little cot in a cubby under the staircase. It's terribly small and not very comfortable—"

"My dear," Uncle Ned told her with a gracious smile. "I'm certain that under the circumstances were it merely a pillow slip stuffed with stones, it should suffice."

She smiled back at him as she slipped her hand into his.

CHAPTER 26

IT WAS ALMOST NOON WHEN UNCLE NED GAVE MIZ Maggie a parting kiss and headed for town. Despite his assurances to her, he had no new plan. He only hoped the sulphate of morphine had finally taken effect on Snade.

But he located the gunman at the railroad station, looking hale and hearty, watching the female passengers depart the midday train.

Stepping to Snade's side, he offered as cordial a greeting as he could manage. Snade grunted in reply, then suddenly poked Uncle Ned in the ribs and pointed toward the caboose. "Look at that!"

Trainmen were rolling a large barrel out of the way car. Uncle Ned looked at it. It seemed a perfectly ordinary barrel.

Snade said, "Don't that keg say *oysters* on it?"

"Indeed it does," Uncle Ned allowed.

"That bastard at the restaurant told me oysters was out of season."

"Indeed they are."

"The hell they are! There's a whole damn keg full of them being delivered fresh!" Snade glared at Uncle Ned as if defying him to deny it.

"Perhaps they're South American oysters," Uncle Ned suggested. "The seasons are different south of the equator, you know."

Snade, unfamiliar with equators, snorted and said, "Dammit, I'm gonna have me a bellyful of them oysters or else. Come on."

The barrel was headed for Ransom's. Snade strode after it, with Uncle Ned tagging along behind. Inside the restaurant, passengers from the train had taken all the tables. Snade picked the table he wanted and unceremoniously evicted its occupants. As he sat down, he motioned for Uncle Ned to join him.

"Hey you!" he hollered at Ransom. "Gimme a big batch of them oysters!"

"Oysters are still out of season," Ransom told him.

"Like hell! I just seen a whole barrel full of 'em being delivered. I want some."

"No, you don't. Not those oysters—"

"Don't tell me what I want!" Snade's gaze narrowed. His upper lip curled. "You got it in for me or something? You saving them oysters for that dumbass Cannonball Kid or something?"

"No," Ransom said. He looked at Uncle Ned.

Uncle Ned shrugged.

Ransom sighed. "If you insist—"

"I insist. A batch for me and a batch for the Colonel here."

"Colonel McGunn, if I were you—" Ransom began.

At the same time, Uncle Ned said, "I'm afraid I'm not hungry."

"*Bring 'em,*" Snade said.

Ransom trotted off to the kitchen. He returned shortly carrying two plates piled high with raw oysters. He set one in front of Snade. As he set the other in front of Uncle Ned he gave a warning shake of his head.

Snade began scooping oysters into his maw.

Uncle Ned took one look at the pale gray-green globs on the plate and pressed a hand to his stomach.

"What's the matter, Colonel?" Snade said. "Go ahead, have some. They're delicious."

Uncle Ned said weakly, "I fear I don't have much of an appetite."

"Have some."

206

"Oysters don't always agree with me."

"I said *have some.*"

Reluctantly, Uncle Ned lifted an oyster and slid it into his mouth. With difficulty, he swallowed. Suddenly he rose. Giving Snade a quick stiff bit of a bow, he gulped, "Excuse me, please!"

Snade grunted. His lips twitched with amusement as he watched Uncle Ned hurry toward the back door. Drawing the second dish toward himself, he muttered, "Damned old ass can't hold his oysters either."

At the door, Ransom grabbed Uncle Ned's arm. "I was trying to warn you—"

"*Not now!*" Uncle Ned gasped. He jerked free of Ransom's hand and dashed for the outhouse.

"Don't eat any of those oysters, Colonel McGunn!" Ransom called after him. "That shipment was lost in transit! It was due here last April!"

Unnerved by the thought of facing either Whip Snade or the oysters again, Uncle Ned lingered in the outhouse far longer than was necessary. He stayed until an insistent pounding at the door and several harsh threats compelled him to vacate it.

Driven by some small hope of coping with Snade in the short time left before the showdown, he forced himself back to the table. He found Shade avidly devouring yet another dish of oysters.

Averting his eyes, he seated himself and asked for black coffee.

He was on his third cup when Snade swallowed a final oyster, belched, rose, rubbed his stomach, belched again, and said, "How about a drink, Colonel?"

Uncle Ned groaned softly. His interest in alcohol was at low ebb this morning. Reluctantly, he mumbled, "Just a short one."

Snade ambled toward The Flying Eagle with Uncle Ned plodding along at his side. In the street in front of the saloon workmen were busy putting the finishing touches on the reviewing stand. Inside the saloon prospective spectators were fortifying themselves for the afternoon's event. Snade elbowed his way up to the bar with Uncle Ned trailing behind him.

The bartender informed them that he was sold out of everything except snake juice. Snade ordered a bottle and two glasses. Uncle Ned groaned slightly.

The snake juice was authentic, with the fangs and button of a rattler in the bottle to prove it. Snade poured four fingers into each glass. Lifting his in toast, he said, "Here's to another notch on my gun."

"Ung," Uncle Ned said politely. Raising his own glass, he touched his tongue to the liquor. Then, manfully, he took a gulp.

Snade emptied his glass, set it on the bar, and reached for the bottle. He hesitated, looking vaguely puzzled. He belched and eyed Uncle Ned. Thoughtfully, he said, "I recollect I seen a medicine wagon over near the depot yesterday."

"Indeed," Uncle Ned said.

"Come on." Snade pushed away from the bar and shoved through the crowd toward the door.

Following him, Uncle Ned asked, "Is something the matter?"

"I think that bastard at the restaurant shucked me. I think them oysters he give me wasn't right fresh or something." Snade seemed bewildered. "I think I got me a bellyache. I ain't never had no bellyache before. I think I got one now."

"Indeed," Uncle Ned said.

The special excursion train bringing in more spectators

for the day's big event had just pulled into the station. It was spewing forth masses of avid tourists.

On the open tailgate of his wagon, the Professor stood in his white frock coat and plug hat. His chin was fresh shaven and his moustache neatly trimmed. Despite a slight redness, his eyes sparkled at the sight of so many potential customers. Snapping on his drum, he began to pound.

By the time Whip Snade and Uncle Ned arrived, a goodly crowd was bunched up around the wagon. Bulling through it, Snade reached the platform.

"Hey you! Medicine man!" he shouted.

The Professor stopped his banging and looked down over his drum. Loudly enough for all the assemblage to hear, he called, "Ah, Mister Whip Snade!"

A murmur of interest ran through the crowd. Several of the people nearest Snade pushed back a step.

"How may I serve you, Mister Snade?" the Professor asked.

"That horsepiss you're selling any good for a bellyache?"

"I can assure you, sir, Doctor Sylvester's marvelous Medicinal Oil is a most remedial specific for alimentary ailments—"

"Answer me *yes* or *no!*"

"Yes."

"Gimme a bottle."

The Professor produced a bottle and held it out. "For an internal discomfort," he said. "The medication should be applied generously over the afflicted member, in this case the abdomen, and massaged gently into the skin—"

Snade snatched a bottle.

"That will be one dollar, please," the Professor said, thrusting an open hand toward him.

Ignoring it, he pocketed the bottle and walked away.

"Sir!" the Professor called. "Sir, you forgot to pay me!"

The audience chortled.

The Professor mumbled something to himself, then forced a professional smile onto his face and turned to present his customary address to the assemblage.

Uncle Ned stood apart in the shadow of the depot watching Snade go. Bellyache or no, the gunman looked not in the least incapacitated.

Uncle Ned felt rather ill himself. But he feared no mere grifter's flukum could aid him in his own dilemma. Not only had he inadvertently placed his young nephew in dire jeopardy, but now he had to face dear Margaret and admit that he'd failed to find a solution to the problem.

CHAPTER 27

THE WORKMEN HAD FINISHED UP AND GONE OFF TO quench their thirsts before the festivities began. Dignitaries were gathering on the bunting-bedecked reviewing stand. Gaily laughing children and adults alike, all in their Sunday finery, lined the street. Many were waving small flags. Some admitted partiality by displaying pennants with symbolic cannonballs or whips emblazoned on them.

Miz Maggie was on the reviewing stand when Uncle Ned arrived. Morosely he mounted the steps toward her, climbing as if to a gallows. She met him with an anxious, "Well?"

He shook his head.

She sunk down into her chair.

Seating himself beside her, he took her hand in his.

He asked, "Where is the boy?"

She gave an indicative nod.

He saw Henry then, chatting with Miss Lavinia in the shade of the Professor's wagon. Henry wore a new outfit of white silk ornamented with polished silver conchos. His massive white sombrero was in his hand. His hair was carefully parted down the center, slicked in place with lilac scented grease. His fresh-scrubbed face was bright, his grin shy, his stance proud.

"Poor child," Miz Maggie sighed.

Uncle Ned patted her hand.

The Mayor stepped to his podium. He took the script of his speech from his pocket and spread it out before him. Gesturing, he caught the bandmaster's eye. The bandmaster called forth a fanfare from the brass. The crowd turned its attention to the reviewing stand.

The Mayor cleared his throat and began his speech. He welcomed the masses of spectators who had come to the Fair And Flourishing City Of Buskin to celebrate the anniversary of the Founding Of This Great Nation, the Emergence Of The United States Of America As A World Power, and the Impending Encounter Between Two Nationally Famous Figures. By the time he finally finished the speech he had completely lost the crowd's attention. The band regained it by blasting out another fanfare.

The crowd looked around expectantly.

Miss Lavinia gave Henry a nudge. He started, remembering where he was and why. For an instant he hesitated. Miss Lavinia smiled at him. He beamed at her, then strode toward the reviewing stand.

The crowd cheered.

Miz Maggie clutched Uncle Ned's hand tighter. He patted it again.

At the far end of the street, Whip Snade appeared. He

211

had changed into his working clothes. He was dressed in black from bootheels to bowler hat to the tips of his kid gloves. He stood for a moment, letting the crowd admire him. Then in a most businesslike manner he stripped off his coat and held it out to a nearby spectator. Awed, the spectator accepted the honor.

Snade's shirt was as black as the coat. He wore bright yellow sleeve garters. With a casual briskness, he removed his gloves and handed them to the spectator. He adjusted the sleeve garters, fingered the ebony butts of his revolvers, then touched his hat brim to his audience.

A rather tense cheer went up.

At his own end of the street, Henry watched Snade with admiration. The gunman sure had style. Henry wished he had something he could take off that way. Lacking anything suitable to peel, he put on his sombrero, then touched the brim of it to the crowd. Another tense cheer rose.

"Gentlemen!" the Mayor called out. "Ready?"

Henry nodded.

Snade belched. "Just a minute," he grumbled. He jerked his coat back from the spectator, fished a bottle from the pocket, and dropped the coat in the street. He took a long draught from the bottle, then slipped it into his hip pocket. He wiped his mouth with the back of his hand, touched his gun butts again, and announced, "Ready!"

"*One!*" the Mayor called.

Henry assumed the crouch so familiar to readers of Colonel Buck McGunn's books.

Snade flexed his fingers.

"*Two!*"

Snade's mouth twitched. A frown creased his

212

forehead. Beads of perspiration popped out on his brow. The color began to fade from his face.

"*Thr—!*"

Snade belched. His knees quivered. He leaned precariously forward. With the majesty of a felled redwood, he toppled face down into the dust.

A murmur of questions rippled through the crowd. People pushed forward to surround the fallen man. Waving a bottle of his marvelous oil, the Professor leaped from the tailgate of his wagon and shouted, "Let me through! I'm a medical man! Let me through!"

Dashing down from the reviewing stand, Uncle Ned shouted, "Everybody stand back! Let the medical man through! Stand back!"

He and the Professor came together at Snade's side. Briskly, Uncle Ned appointed several husky spectators to hold the crowd back, well away from the fallen gunman.

The Professor dropped to his knees. Uncle Ned knelt next to him. They rolled Snade onto his back. His face was distorted, the mouth agape, the eyes wide, the flesh an oysterish gray green.

"He's dead," Uncle Ned surmised.

The Professor nodded professional agreement. He said, "Of what?"

"I can think of any number of possible causes," Uncle Ned whispered. His hand slid surreptitiously under the corpse's rump. It came out again partially concealing a half empty bottle. As Uncle Ned slipped the bottle into his own pocket, the Professor spotted it.

"My flukum?"

"Indeed." Uncle Ned rose to his feet. Turning slowly, he looked into the expectant faces of the spectators. He removed his hat, placed it against his chest, and said solemnly, "No man but The Cannonball Kid himself could possibly strike such fear into an opponent's heart as to cause that member to forthwith cease its functioning."

"Beautiful," the Professor murmured. Rising, he addressed the assemblage. "I regret to admit that even so miraculous a curative as Doctor Sylvester's Marvelous Medicinal Oil is incapable of raising the dead."

Henry struggled through the crowd with Miss Lavinia in tow. Peering at his uncle, he asked, "He's *dead?*"

"Indeed he is, my boy. To all appearances, he has succumbed to fright at the mere sight of you."

Miss Lavinia flung her arms around Henry's neck.

He turned red.

The crowd cheered.

"Strike up the band!" the Mayor shouted.

Suddenly the town telegrapher was shoving through the crowd. Thrusting a folded slip of paper at the Mayor, he gasped out several words. The blare of the band drowned them.

The Mayor opened the paper, perused it, then rushed back to the reviewing stand. Pounding on the podium, he got the bandmaster's attention. The music stopped. The crowd quieted down.

The Mayor waved the paper. "This telegram just arrived! It's from the world famous gunfighter, Rudy Hogg! Mister Hogg says he's on his way to Buskin to face the winner of today's showdown! He'll arrive on the noon train tomorrow!"

The crowd cheered.

Miss Lavinia sighed, "Oh Cannonball! I'm so proud of you!"

Henry grinned.

Miz Maggie fainted.

CHAPTER 28

ONCE AGAIN, THE RED LANTERN IN FRONT OF MIZ Maggie's offered no welcome to wayfarers in the night.

The single small lamp in the parlor gave form to three figures. Miz Maggie and Uncle Ned sat on a love seat, their fingers entwined. The Professor stood by the sideboard, refilling glasses.

"By the way," he said. "Where is Henry now?"

"The poor boy came straight home after the shootout," Miz Maggie answered. "He must have been tuckered out after his ordeal. He asked me if he could use my room again. I imagine he's sound asleep now."

"I trust no one is using the cubby under the stairs," Uncle Ned said.

"Neddy dear," Miz Maggie told, him. "I couldn't care less."

"*Margaret!*"

"Neddy, I am exhausted. I cannot stand going through all this again. I cannot possibly face another showdown between that poor child and some vicious killer. We *have* to do something."

"We shall my dear."

Passing out the drinks, the Professor suggested, "Why not just get him out of town?"

"I've tried!" Miz Maggie said. "I've tried over and over again. He refuses to go. The poor dear has such a strong sense of honor and obligation."

The Professor muttered something to himself and settled into a chair. For a while, all drank in thoughtful silence. When he'd emptied his glass, the Professor got to his feet again. "If you have no further need of me, I do have something pending back at my wagon."

"If we need you, we'll send for you," Miz Maggie told him.

"No! Please, no. For God's sake, *don't* come banging on my door in the middle of everything again!"

"Go ahead, Clarence," Uncle Ned said. "Go. Take your pleasure. Forget our dire need. Forget that poor boy who faces certain death on the morrow."

The Professor loosed a long and mournful sigh. He turned to the sideboard to refill his glass.

Suddenly Uncle Ned sprung to his feet. "I've got it!"

"What?" Miz Maggie asked.

"May I go now?" the Professor said.

"Come along with me!" Uncle Ned grabbed the lamp and bounded up the stairs with Miz Maggie and the Professor close behind him.

The door to Miz Maggie's bedroom was shut. He tried the knob. It was latched. He rapped. There was no answer. He rapped again. Nothing.

"The poor weary child," Miz Maggie said. "It's a pity to disturb him."

"Indeed," Uncle Ned grunted as he hauled off and gave the door a thorough banging.

At last there was a response. From within, Henry groaned, "What's the matter?"

Uncle Ned called back, "We must speak to you, boy!"

"Can't it wait until morning?"

"No."

"Is the house on fire?"

"No."

"Then why can't it wait until morning?"

"Believe me, boy, it is most imperative that we discuss this matter *now!*"

"All right," Henry sighed. "Just a minute."

Eventually the door inched open. Henry peered out

216

through the narrow crack. "What is it, Uncle Ned?"

"Let us in. This is a matter of life and death." Uncle Ned shoved against the door.

Reluctantly, Henry stepped back and let them in.

Lifting the lamp high, Uncle Ned declaimed, "I have had an inspiration. A stroke of genius. A true enlightenment—"

"Get on with it, Neddy," the Professor grumbled.

Uncle Ned glared at him. "Clarence, please do not call me that."

"Get on with it, Neddy dear," Miz Maggie said.

"Yes, dear. As I was saying, I have had an inspiration. My boy," he looked at Henry. "Your career as a gunfighter has reached its climax today. Now, you must move on to greater glory. You must retire from the field. Hang up your guns as it were, and give yourself to your public."

"Sir?"

"You are undoubtedly familiar with the success of that hunter, Cody, in such theatrical vehicles as *Buffalo Bill: The King Of The Border Men,* and *Scouts Of The Plains.*"

Miz Maggie and the Professor nodded. Henry shook his head.

"Indeed, boy?" Uncle Ned said. "Certainly you must have heard of Buffalo Bill Cody?"

"Yes, sir, he's in books, like me, only you didn't write them."

"Would that I had. However, that is neither here nor there. It happens that Cody also treads the boards in the flesh. He has performed to avid audiences throughout the nation. The people hunger to actually see and hear their heroes. It should be but the work of a moment to produce a play script based on the deeds of The Cannonball Kid."

He turned to Miz Maggie. "My dear Margaret, would

217

you consider accompanying us in this venture?"

"I'd go to the ends of the earth with you, Neddy dear."

Henry said, "I don't want to go now. Besides, I got to shoot Mister Hogg tomorrow."

"Neddy," Miz Maggie said. "Suppose Hogg decides to follow us and challenge Cannonball again?"

"Impossible. Once the boy has made a public declaration of his retirement from such affairs, no one can honorably offer him such a challenge. Once he has made his commitment to his public, he can hardly accept such a challenge with honor."

"Honor?" Henry said uncertainly.

Uncle Ned nodded. "Not merely honor, my boy, but duty as well. It is your obligation to give the American Public the opportunity to behold you in all your living splendor."

"Uh—" Henry glanced thoughtfully around the room. Slowly, he allowed, "I reckon if it's my duty I got to do it."

"Indeed!" Uncle Ned smiled. "Clarence, perhaps we can prevail on you for transportation to some convenient point?"

"I *had* plans for this evening," the Professor said.

"I'll go," Henry said. "Only I ain't going alone. I'm taking Miss Lavinia with me."

"What?"

A sudden scraping sounded. All eyes turned toward the massive wardrobe trunk in the corner. The lid was slowly rising. A figure emerged. Miss Lavinia, clad in her petticoats.

"Henry!" Miz Maggie gasped.

Uncle Ned grunted, "What the devil?"

The Professor lifted a brow at Henry. "Congratulations, my lad."

218

Turning red, Henry mumbled, "We're gonna get married."

Miss Lavinia climbed out of the trunk. Brushing at her rumpled petticoats, she said, "Colonel McGunn, I've always wanted to go on the stage. Please, couldn't you write a part for me into your play?"

"Call me Uncle Ned, my dear. Of course I can put in a part for you. Indeed, every story should have its touch of romance, should it not?"

"Yeah," Henry said, taking Miss Lavinia's hand in his.

Uncle Ned continued, "We can climax the production with the young lovers declaring their betrothal."

The Professor suggested, "Why not have an actual marriage ceremony on stage?"

"Excellent! Run fetch your wagon, Clarence, and we'll be off!" Uncle Ned turned to Miz Maggie. "Marriage is indeed the proper ending for my story."

Miz Maggie nodded. Slipping her hand into his, she said, "Yes indeed, Neddy dear."

We hope that you enjoyed reading this
Sagebrush Large Print Western. If you would like to
read more Sagebrush titles, ask your
librarian or contact the Publishers:

United States and Canada
Thomas T. Beeler, *Publisher*
Post Office Box 659
Hampton Falls, New Hampshire 03844-0659
(800) 818-7574

**United Kingdom, Eire, and
the Republic of South Africa**
Isis Publishing Ltd
7 Centremead
Osney Mead
Oxford OX2 0ES England
(01865) 250333

Australia and New Zealand
Bolinda Publishing Pty. Ltd.
17 Mohr Street
Tullamarine, 3043, Victoria, Australia
(016103) 9338 0666